I0661101

Henry Howard Brownell

War-lyrics

And other Poems

Henry Howard Brownell

War-lyrics
And other Poems

ISBN/EAN: 9783744787055

Printed in Europe, USA, Canada, Australia, Japan

Cover: Foto ©Andreas Hilbeck / pixelio.de

More available books at **www.hansebooks.com**

WAR-LYRICS

AND OTHER POEMS.

BY

HENRY HOWARD BROWNELL.

BOSTON:
TICKNOR AND FIELDS.
1866.

TO

THE VICE-ADMIRAL,

DAVID GLASGOW FARRAGUT.

Sir, —

Permit me to inscribe to you this book, a part of which is due to the inspiration of your deeds and your example.

What you have been in war is known to your country, to her enemies, and to the world ; but only those who have had the honor of approaching you nearly can know how great is your love for peace, how real your kindliness, how true your feeling for nature, your interest in art, letters, and science, how genial, even in the roughest times, your sense of wit and humor and of all the amenities of social life.

It is in remembrance of these traits, and of the personal friendship you were pleased to accord me while serving under your command, that I once again write myself,

Very respectfully,

Your obedient servant,

THE AUTHOR.

CONTENTS.

MISCELLANEOUS POEMS.

EARLY POEMS.

THE BAY FIGHT.

(MOBILE BAY, AUGUST 5, 1864.)

"On the forecastle, Ulf the Red
  Watched the lashing of the ships —
'If the Serpent lie so far ahead,
  We shall have hard work of it here,'
    Said he."

LONGFELLOW's "*Saga of King Olaf.*"

THREE days through sapphire seas we sailed,
  The steady Trade blew strong and free,
The Northern Light his banners paled,
The Ocean Stream our channels wet,
  We rounded low Canaveral's lee,
And passed the isles of emerald set
  In blue Bahama's turquoise sea.

By reef and shoal obscurely mapped,
  And hauntings of the gray sea-wolf,
The palmy Western Key lay lapped
  In the warm washing of the Gulf.

But weary to the hearts of all
  The burning glare, the barren reach
  Of Santa Rosa's withered beach,
And Pensacola's ruined wall.

1   A

And weary was the long patrol,
   The thousand miles of shapeless strand,
From Brazos to San Blas that roll
   Their drifting dunes of desert sand.

Yet, coast-wise as we cruised or lay,
   The land-breeze still at nightfall bore,
By beach and fortress-guarded bay,
   Sweet odors from the enemy's shore,

Fresh from the forest solitudes,
   Unchallenged of his sentry lines —
The bursting of his cypress buds,
   And the warm fragrance of his pines.

Ah, never braver bark and crew,
   Nor bolder Flag a foe to dare,
Had left a wake on ocean blue
   Since Lion-Heart sailed *Trenc-le-mer !*[1]

But little gain by that dark ground
   Was ours, save, sometime, freer breath
For friend or brother strangely found,
   'Scaped from the drear domain of death.

And little venture for the bold,
   Or laurel for our valiant Chief,
   Save some blockaded British thief,
Full fraught with murder in his hold,

Caught unawares at ebb or flood —
  Or dull bombardment, day by day,
  With fort and earth-work, far away,
Low couched in sullen leagues of mud.

A weary time, — but to the strong
  The day at last, as ever, came;
And the volcano, laid so long,
  Leaped forth in thunder and in flame!

"Man your starboard battery!"
  Kimberly shouted —
The ship, with her hearts of oak,
Was going, mid roar and smoke,
    On to victory!
  None of us doubted,
  No, not our dying —
  Farragut's Flag was flying!

Gaines growled low on our left,
  Morgan roared on our right —
Before us, gloomy and fell,
With breath like the fume of hell,
Lay the Dragon of iron shell,
  Driven at last to the fight!

Ha, old ship! do they thrill,
  The brave two hundred scars
  You got in the River-Wars?
That were leeched with clamorous skill,

(Surgery savage and hard,)
Splinted with bolt and beam,
Probed in scarfing and seam,
 Rudely linted and tarred
With oakum and boiling pitch,
And sutured with splice and hitch,
 At the Brooklyn Navy-Yard!

Our lofty spars were down,
To bide the battle's frown,
(Wont of old renown)—
But every ship was drest
In her bravest and her best,
 As if for a July day;
Sixty flags and three,
 As we floated up the bay—
Every peak and mast-head flew
The brave Red, White, and Blue—
 We were eighteen ships that day.

With hawsers strong and taut,
The weaker lashed to port,
 On we sailed, two by two—
That if either a bolt should feel
Crash through caldron or wheel,
Fin of bronze or sinew of steel,
 Her mate might bear her through.

Steadily nearing the head,
The great Flag-Ship led,

Grandest of sights !
On her lofty mizen flew
Our Leader's dauntless Blue,
    That had waved o'er twenty fights —
So we went, with the first of the tide,
    Slowly, mid the roar
    Of the Rebel guns ashore
And the thunder of each full broadside.

Ah, how poor the prate
Of statute and state
    We once held with these fellows —
Here, on the flood's pale-green,
    Hark how he bellows,
    Each bluff old Sea-Lawyer !
Talk to them, Dahlgren,
    Parrott, and Sawyer !

On, in the whirling shade
    Of the cannon's sulphury breath,
    We drew to the Line of Death
That our devilish Foe had laid —
Meshed in a horrible net,
    And baited villanous well,
Right in our path were set
    Three hundred traps of hell !

And there, O sight forlorn !
    There, while the cannon
        Hurtled and thundered —
    (Ah, what ill raven

Flapped o'er the ship that morn!) —
Caught by the under-death,
In the drawing of a breath
   Down went dauntless Craven,
     He and his hundred !

A moment we saw her turret,
   A little heel she gave,
And a thin white spray went o'er her,
   Like the crest of a breaking wave —
In that great iron coffin,
   The channel for their grave,
   The fort their monument,
(Seen afar in the offing,)
Ten fathom deep lie Craven,
   And the bravest of our brave.

Then, in that deadly track,
A little the ships held back,
   Closing up in their stations —
There are minutes that fix the fate
   Of battles and of nations,
   (Christening the generations,)
When valor were all too late,
   If a moment's doubt be harbored —
From the main-top, bold and brief,
Came the word of our grand old Chief —
   "Go on !" 'twas all he said —
Our helm was put to starboard,
   And the Hartford passed ahead.

Ahead lay the Tennessee,
  On our starboard bow he lay,
With his mail-clad consorts three,
  (The rest had run up the Bay) —
There he was, belching flame from his bow,
And the steam from his throat's abyss
Was a Dragon's maddened hiss —
  In sooth a most curséd craft ! —
In a sullen ring at bay
By the Middle Ground they lay,
  Raking us fore and aft.

  Trust me, our berth was hot,
  Ah, wickedly well they shot ;
How their death-bolts howled and stung !
  And the water-batteries played
  With their deadly cannonade
Till the air around us rung ;
So the battle raged and roared —
Ah, had you been aboard
  To have seen the fight we made !

How they leaped, the tongues of flame,
  From the cannon's fiery lip !
How the broadsides, deck and frame,
  Shook the great ship !

And how the enemy's shell
  Came crashing, heavy and oft,
  Clouds of splinters flying aloft

And falling in oaken showers —
  But ah, the pluck of the crew !
Had you stood on that deck of ours,
· You had seen what men may do.

Still, as the fray grew louder,
  Boldly they worked and well ;
Steadily came the powder,
  Steadily came the shell.
And if tackle or truck found hurt,
  Quickly they cleared the wreck ;
And the dead were laid to port,
  All a-row, on our deck.

  Never a nerve that failed,
  Never a cheek that paled,
Not a tinge of gloom or pallor —
  There was bold Kentucky's grit,
And the old Virginian valor,
  And the daring Yankee wit.

There were blue eyes from turfy Shannon,
  There were black orbs from palmy Niger —
But there, alongside the cannon,
  Each man fought like a tiger !

A little, once, it looked ill,
  Our consort began to burn —
They quenched the flames with a will,
But our men were falling still,
  And still the fleet was astern.

Right abreast of the Fort
  In an awful shroud they lay,
  Broadsides thundering away,
And lightning from every port —
  Scene of glory and dread !
A storm-cloud all aglow
  With flashes of fiery red —
The thunder raging below,
  And the forest of flags o'erhead !

So grand the hurly and roar,
  So fiercely their broadsides blazed,
The regiments fighting ashore
  Forgot to fire as they gazed.

  There, to silence the Foe,
  Moving grimly and slow,
They loomed in that deadly wreath,
  Where the darkest batteries frowned —
  Death in the air all round,
And the black torpedoes beneath !

And now, as we looked ahead,
  All for'ard, the long white deck
Was growing a strange dull red ;
  But soon, as once and agen
Fore and aft we sped,
  (The firing to guide or check,)
You could hardly choose but tread
  On the ghastly human wreck,

(Dreadful gobbet and shred
   That a minute ago were men!)

Red, from main-mast to bitts!
  Red, on bulwark and wale —
Red, by combing and hatch —
  Red, o'er netting and rail!

And ever, with steady con,
  The ship forged slowly by —
And ever the crew fought on,
  And their cheers rang loud and high.

Grand was the sight to see
   How by their guns they stood,
Right in front of our dead
  Fighting square abreast —
Each brawny arm and chest
All spotted with black and red,
   Chrism of fire and blood!

Worth our watch, dull and sterile,
  Worth all the weary time —
Worth the woe and the peril,
  To stand in that strait sublime!

Fear? A forgotten form!
  Death? A dream of the eyes!
We were atoms in God's great storm
  That roared through the angry skies.

One only doubt was ours,
   One only dread we knew —
Could the day that dawned so well
Go down for the Darker Powers?
   Would the fleet get through?
And ever the shot and shell
Came with the howl of hell,
The splinter-clouds rose and fell,
   And the long line of corpses grew —
   Would the fleet win through?

They are men that never will fail,
   (How aforetime they 've fought!)
But Murder may yet prevail —
      They may sink as Craven sank.
   Therewith one hard, fierce thought,
Burning on heart and lip,
Ran like fire through the ship —
   Fight her, to the last plank!

A dimmer Renown might strike
   If Death lay square alongside —
But the Old Flag has no like,
   She must fight, whatever betide —
When the War is a tale of old,
And this day's story is told,
   They shall hear how the Hartford died!

But as we ranged ahead,
   And the leading ships worked in,

Losing their hope to win
The enemy turned and fled —
And one seeks a shallow reach,
  And another, winged in her flight,
  Our mate, brave Jouett, brings in —
  And one, all torn in the fight,
Runs for a wreck on the beach,
  Where her flames soon fire the night.

And the Ram, when well up the Bay,
  And we looked that our stems should meet,
(He had us fair for a prey,)
Shifting his helm midway,
  Sheered off and ran for the fleet ;
There, without skulking or sham,
  He fought them, gun for gun,
And ever·he sought to ram,
  But could finish never a one.

From the first of the iron shower
  Till we sent our parting shell,
'Twas just one savage hour
  Of the roar and the rage of hell.

With the lessening smoke and thunder,
  Our glasses around we aim —
What is that burning yonder?
  Our Philippi, — aground and in flame !

Below, 'twas still all a-roar,
As the ships went by the shore,

But the fire of the Fort had slacked,
(So fierce their volleys had been) —
And now, with a mighty din,
The whole fleet came grandly in,
  Though sorely battered and wracked.

So, up the Bay we ran,
  The Flag to port and ahead ;
And a pitying rain began
  To wash the lips of our dead.

A league from the Fort we lay,
  And deemed that the end must lag ;
When lo ! looking down the Bay,
  There flaunted the Rebel Rag —
The Ram is again underway
  And heading dead for the Flag !

Steering up with the stream,
  Boldly his course he lay,
Though the fleet all answered his fire,
And, as he still drew nigher,
  Ever on bow and beam
    Our Monitors pounded away —
    How the Chicasaw hammered away !

Quickly breasting the wave,
  Eager the prize to win,
First of us all the brave

Monongahela went in
Under full head of steam —
Twice she struck him abeam,
Till her stem was a sorry work,
   (She might have run on a crag!)
The Lackawana hit fair,
He flung her aside like cork,
   And still he held for the Flag.

High in the mizen shroud,
   (Lest the smoke his sight o'erwhelm,)
Our Admiral's voice rang loud,
   " Hard-a-starboard your helm!
Starboard! and run him down!"
   Starboard it was — and so,
Like a black squall's lifting frown,
Our mighty bow bore down
   On the iron beak of the Foe.

We stood on the deck together,
   Men that had looked on death
In battle and stormy weather —
   Yet a little we held our breath,
   When, with the hush of death,
The great ships drew together.

Our Captain strode to the bow,
   Drayton, courtly and wise,
   Kindly cynic, and wise,
(You hardly had known him now,
   The flame of fight in his eyes!)

His brave heart eager to feel
How the oak would tell on the steel!

But, as the space grew short,
 A little he seemed to shun us,
Out peered a form grim and lanky,
 And a voice yelled — " Hard-a-port!
Hard-a-port! — here 's the damned Yankee
 Coming right down on us!"

He sheered, but the ships ran foul
With a gnarring shudder and growl —
 He gave us a deadly gun;
But as he passed in his pride,
(Rasping right alongside!)
 The Old Flag, in thunder tones,
Poured in her port broadside,
Rattling his iron hide,
 And cracking his timber bones!

Just then, at speed on the Foe,
 With her bow all weathered and brown,
 The great Lackawana came down,
Full tilt, for another blow;
We were forging ahead,
 She reversed — but, for all our pains,
Rammed the old Hartford, instead,
 Just for'ard the mizzen chains!

Ah! how the masts did buckle and bend,
 And the stout hull ring and reel,

As she took us right on end!
  (Vain were engine and wheel,
  She was under full steam) —
With the roar of a thunder-stroke
Her two thousand tons of oak
  Brought up on us, right abeam!

A wreck, as it looked, we lay —
(Rib and plankshear gave way
  To the stroke of that giant wedge!)
Here, after all, we go —
The old ship is gone! — ah, no,
  But cut to the water's edge.

Never mind, then — at him again!
  His flurry now can't last long;
He 'll never again see land —
Try that on *him*, Marchand!
  On him again, brave Strong!

Heading square at the hulk,
  Full on his beam we bore;
But the spine of the huge Sea-Hog
Lay on the tide like a log,
  He vomited flame no more.

By this, he had found it hot —
  Half the fleet, in an angry ring,
  Closed round the hideous Thing,
Hammering with solid shot,
And bearing down, bow on bow —

He has but a minute to choose ;
Life or renown ? — which now
　　Will the Rebel Admiral lose?

Cruel, haughty, and cold,
He ever was strong and bold —
　　Shall he shrink from a wooden stem ?
He will think of that brave band
He sank in the Cumberland —
　　Aye, he will sink like them.

Nothing left but to fight
Boldly his last sea-fight !
　　Can he strike ?　By heaven, 'tis true !
　　Down comes the traitor Blue,
And up goes the captive White !

Up went the White !　Ah then
The hurrahs that, once and agen,
Rang from three thousand men
　　All flushed and savage with fight !
Our dead lay cold and stark,　·
But our dying, down in the dark,
　　Answered as best they might —
Lifting their poor lost arms,
　　And cheering for God and Right !

Ended the mighty noise,
　　Thunder of forts and ships.
　　　Down we went to the hold —
O, our dear dying boys !

B

How we pressed their poor brave lips,
  (Ah, so pallid and cold!)
And held their hands to the last,
  (Those that had hands to hold).

Still thee, O woman heart!
  (So strong an hour ago)—
If the idle tears must start,
  'Tis not in vain they flow.

They died, our children dear,
  On the drear berth deck they died;
Do not think of them here—
Even now their footsteps near
The immortal, tender sphere—
(Land of love and cheer!
  Home of the Crucified!)

And the glorious deed survives.
  Our threescore, quiet and cold,
Lie thus, for a myriad lives
  And treasure-millions untold—
(Labor of poor men's lives,
Hunger of weans and wives,
  Such is war-wasted gold.)

Our ship and her fame to-day
  Shall float on the storied Stream,
When mast and shroud have crumbled away
  And her long white deck is a dream.

One daring leap in the dark,
   Three mortal hours, at the most—
And hell lies stiff and stark
   On a hundred leagues of coast.

For the mighty Gulf is ours—
    The Bay is lost and won,
    An Empire is lost and won!
Land, if thou yet hast flowers,
Twine them in one more wreath
   Of tenderest white and red,
('Twin buds of glory and death!)
    For the brows of our brave dead—
    For thy Navy's noblest Son.

Joy, O Land, for thy sons,
   Victors by flood and field!
The traitor walls and guns
   Have nothing left but to yield—
   (Even now they surrender!)

And the ships shall sail once more,
   And the cloud of war sweep on
To break on the cruel shore—
   But Craven is gone,
   He and his hundred are gone.

The flags flutter up and down
   At sunrise and twilight dim,

The cannons menace and frown —
　　But never again for him,
　　Him and the hundred.

The Dahlgrens are dumb,
　　Dumb are the mortars —
Never more shall the drum
　　Beat to colors and quarters —
　　The great guns are silent.

O brave heart and loyal !
　　Let all your colors dip —
　　Mourn him, proud Ship !
From main deck to royal.
　　God rest our Captain,
　　Rest our lost hundred.

Droop, flag and pennant !
　　What is your pride for ?
　　Heaven, that he died for,
Rest our Lieutenant,
　　Rest our brave threescore.

O Mother Land ! this weary life
　　We led, we lead, is 'long of thee ;
Thine the strong agony of strife,
　　And thine the lonely sea.

Thine the long decks all slaughter-sprent,
　　The weary rows of cots that lie

With wrecks of strong men, marred and rent,
  'Neath Pensacola's sky.

And thine the iron caves and dens
  Wherein the flame our war-fleet drives;
The fiery vaults, whose breath is men's
  Most dear and precious lives.

Ah, ever, when with storm sublime
  Dread Nature clears our murky air,
Thus in the crash of falling crime
  Some lesser guilt must share.

Full red the furnace fires must glow
  That melt the ore of mortal kind:
The Mills of God are grinding slow,
  But ah, how close they grind!

To-day the Dahlgren and the drum
  Are dread Apostles of his Name;
His Kingdom here can only come
  By chrism of blood and flame.

Be strong: already slants the gold
  Athwart these wild and stormy skies;
From out this blackened waste, behold,
  What happy homes shall rise!

But see thou well no traitor gloze,
  No striking hands with Death and Shame,
Betray the sacred blood that flows
  So freely for thy name.

And never fear a victor foe —
　　Thy children's hearts are strong and high ;
Nor mourn too fondly — well they know
　　On deck or field to die.

Nor shalt thou want one willing breath,
　　Though, ever smiling round the brave,
The blue sea bear us on to death,
　　The green were one wide grave.

U. S. Flag Ship Hartford, Mobile Bay,
　　　　August, 1864.

THE RIVER FIGHT.

(Mississippi River, April 24, 1862.)

Do you know of the dreary Land,
    If land such region may seem,
Where 'tis neither sea nor strand,
Ocean nor good dry land,
    But the nightmare marsh of a dream —
Where the Mighty River his death-road takes,
'Mid pools, and windings that coil like snakes,
(A hundred leagues of bayous and lakes,)
    To die in the great Gulf Stream?

No coast-line clear and true,
(Granite and deep sea blue,)
    On that dismal shore you pass —
Surf-worn boulder nor sandy beach,
But ooze-flats far as the eye can reach,
    With shallows of water-grass —
Reedy savannas, vast and dun,
Lying dead in the dim March sun —
Huge rotting trunks and roots that lie
Like blackened bones of the Shapes gone by,
    And miles of sunken morass.

No lovely, delicate thing
  Of life o'er the waste is seen —
But the cayman couched by his weedy spring,
  And the pelican, bird unclean —
Or the buzzard, flapping on heavy wing
  Like an evil ghost, o'er the desolate scene.

Ah, many a weary day
With our Leader there we lay,
  In the sultry haze and smoke,
Tugging our ships o'er the bar —
Till the Spring was wasted far,
  Till his brave heart almost broke —
For the sullen River seemed
As if our intent he dreamed —
  All his shallow mouths did spew and choke.

But, ere April fully past,
All ground over at last,
And we knew the die was cast —
  Knew the day drew nigh
To dare to the end one stormy deed,
Might save the Land at her sorest need,
  Or on the old deck to die !

.

Anchored we lay — and, a morn the more,
  To his captains and all his men
Thus wrote our stout old Commodore —
  (He wasn't Admiral then :)

GENERAL ORDERS.

" Send your to'gallant masts down,
   Rig in each flying jib-boom !
   Clear all ahead for the loom
Of traitor fortress and town,
Or traitor fleet bearing down.

   In with your canvas high —
   We shall want no sail to fly !
Topsail and foresail, spanker and jib,
(With the heart of oak in the oaken rib,)
   Shall serve us to win or die !

   Trim every hull by the head,
   (So shall you spare the lead,)
Lest, if she ground, your ship swing round,
   Bows in-shore, for a wreck —
See your grapnels all clear, with pains,
And a solid kedge in your port main-chains,
   With a whip to the main-yard —
   Drop it, heavy and hard,
     When you grapple a traitor deck !

On forecastle and on poop
   Mount guns, as best you may deem —
If possible, rouse them up,
   (For still you must bow the stream) —
Also hoist and secure with stops
Howitzers firmly in your tops,
   To fire on the foe abeam.

Look well to your pumps and hose —
    Have water-tubs, fore and aft,
    For quenching flame in your craft,
      And the gun-crews' fiery thirst —
See planks with felt fitted close,
    To plug every shot-hole tight —
      Stand ready to meet the worst!
    For, if I have reckoned aright,
They will serve us shot, both cold and hot,
    Freely enough, to-night.

Mark well each signal I make —
(Our life-long service at stake,
    And honor that must not lag!)
Whate'er the peril and awe,
In the battle's fieriest flaw,
Let never one ship withdraw
    Till orders come from the Flag!"

Would you hear of the River-Fight?
It was two, of a soft spring night —
    God's stars looked down on all,
And all was clear and bright
But the low fog's chilling breath —
Up the River of Death
    Sailed the Great Admiral.

On our high poop-deck he stood,
    And round him ranged the men

Who have made their birthright good
  Of manhood, once and agen —
Lords of helm and of sail,
Tried in tempest and gale,
  Bronzed in battle and wreck —
Bell and Bailey grandly led
Each his Line of the Blue and Red —
Wainwright stood by our starboard rail,
  Thornton fought the deck.

And I mind me of more than they,
  Of the youthful, steadfast ones,
  That have shown them worthy sons
Of the Seamen passed away —
(Tyson conned our helm, that day,
  Watson stood by his guns.)

What thought our Admiral, then,
Looking down on his men?
  Since the terrible day,
    (Day of renown and tears!)
  When at anchor the Essex lay,
  Holding her foes at bay,
When, a boy, by Porter's side he stood
Till deck and plank-shear were dyed with blood,
    'Tis half a hundred years —
  Half a hundred years, to-day!

Who could fail, with him?
Who reckon of life or limb?
  Not a pulse but beat the higher!

There had you seen, by the star-light dim,
Five hundred faces strong and grim —
   The Flag is going under fire !
Right up by the fort, with her helm hard-a-port,
   The Hartford is going under fire !

The way to our work was plain,
Caldwell had broken the chain,
(Two hulks swung down amain,
   Soon as 'twas sundered) —
Under the night's dark blue,
Steering steady and true,
Ship after ship went through —
Till, as we hove in view,
   Jackson out-thundered.

Back echoed Philip ! — ah, then,
Could you have seen our men,
   How they sprung, in the dim night haze,
To their work of toil and of clamor !
How the loaders, with sponge and rammer,
And their captains, with cord and hammer,
   Kept every muzzle ablaze !
How the guns, as with cheer and shout
Our tackle-men hurled them out,
   Brought up on the water-ways !

First, as we fired at their flash,
   'Twas lightning and black eclipse,
With a bellowing roll and crash —

But soon, upon either bow,
    What with forts, and fire-rafts, and ships —
(The whole fleet was hard at it, now,
All pounding away !) — and Porter
Still thundering with shell and mortar —
    'Twas the mighty sound and form
    Of an Equatorial storm !

(Such you see in the Far South,
After long heat and drouth,
    As day draws nigh to even —
Arching from North to South,
        Blinding the tropic sun,
        The great black bow comes on —
    Till the thunder-veil is riven,
    When all is crash and levin,
    And the cannonade of heaven
        Rolls down the Amazon !)

But, as we worked along higher,
    Just where the river enlarges,
Down came a pyramid of fire —
    It was one of your long coal barges.
    (We had often had the like before) —
'Twas coming down on us to larboard,
    Well in with the eastern shore —
    And our pilot, to let it pass round,
    (You may guess we never stopped to sound,)
Giving us a rank sheer to starboard,
    Ran the Flag hard and fast aground !

'Twas nigh abreast of the Upper Fort,
    And straightway a rascal Ram
    (She was shaped like the devil's dam)
Puffed away for us, with a snort,
    And shoved it, with spiteful strength,
Right alongside of us, to port —
    It was all of our ship's length,
A huge crackling Cradle of the Pit,
    Pitch-pine knots to the brim,
    Belching flame red and grim —
What a roar came up from it!

Well, for a little it looked bad —
        But these things are, somehow, shorter
In the acting than the telling —
There was no singing-out nor yelling,
Nor any fussing and fretting,
        No stampede, in short —
But there we were, my lad,
        All a-fire on our port quarter!
Hammocks a-blaze in the netting,
        Flame spouting in at every port —
Our Fourth Cutter burning at the davit,
(No chance to lower away and save it.)

In a twinkling, the flames had risen
Half way to main top and mizzen,
    Darting up the shrouds like snakes!
    Ah, how we clanked at the brakes,
        And the deep steam-pumps throbbed under,

Sending a ceaseless flow —
Our top-men, a dauntless crowd,
Swarmed in rigging and shroud —
   There, ('twas a wonder !)
The burning ratlins and strands
They quenched with their bare hard hands —
   But the great guns below
   Never silenced their thunder !

At last, by backing and sounding,
When we were clear of grounding,
   And under head-way once more,
The whole rebel fleet came rounding
   The point —— if we had it hot before,
   'Twas now, from shore to shore,
   One long, loud thundering roar —
Such crashing, splintering, and pounding,
   And smashing as you never heard before !

But that we fought foul wrong to wreck,
   And to save the Land we loved so well,
You might have deemed our long gun deck
   Two hundred feet of hell !

For all above was battle,
Broadside, and blaze, and rattle,
   Smoke and thunder alone —
(But, down in the sick-bay,
Where our wounded and dying lay,
   There was scarce a sob or a moan.)

And at last, when the dim day broke,
And the sullen sun awoke,
· Drearily blinking
O'er the haze and the cannon-smoke,
That ever such morning dulls —
There were thirteen traitor hulls
    On fire and sinking!

Now, up the river! — though mad Chalmette
Sputters a vain resistance yet.
Small helm we gave her, our course to steer --
    'Twas nicer work than you well would dream,
With cant and sheer to keep her clear
    Of the burning wrecks that cumbered the stream.

The Louisiana, hurled on high,
Mounts in thunder to meet the sky!
Then down to the depth of the turbid flood,
Fifty fathom of rebel mud!
The Mississippi comes floating down,
A mighty bonfire, from off the town —
And along the river, on stocks and ways,
A half-hatched devil's brood is a-blaze —
The great Anglo-Norman is all in flames,'
(Hark to the roar of her tumbling frames!)
And the smaller fry that Treason would spawn,
Are lighting Algiers like an angry dawn!

From stem to stern, how the pirates burn,
    Fired by the furious hands that built!
So to ashes forever turn
    The suicide wrecks of wrong and guilt!

But, as we neared the city,
  By field and vast plantation,
  (Ah, mill-stone of our Nation!)
With wonder and with pity
  What crowds we there espied
Of dark and wistful faces,
Mute in their toiling-places,
  Strangely and sadly eyed —
  Haply, 'mid doubt and fear,
  Deeming deliverance near —
  (One gave the ghost of a cheer!)

And on that dolorous strand,
  To greet the victor-brave
  One flag did welcome wave —
Raised, ah me! by a wretched hand,
All outworn on our cruel Land —
  The withered hand of a slave!

But all along the Levee,
  In a dark and drenching rain,
(By this, 'twas pouring heavy,)
  Stood a fierce and sullen train —
A strange and a frenzied time!
  There were scowling rage and pain,
    Curses, howls, and hisses,
    Out of hate's black abysses —
Their courage and their crime
  All in vain — all in vain!

For from the hour that the Rebel Stream,
With the Crescent City lying abeam,
   Shuddered under our keel,
Smit to the heart with self-struck sting,
Slavery died in her scorpion-ring,
   And Murder fell on his steel.

'Tis well to do and dare —
But ever may grateful prayer
Follow, as aye it ought,
When the good fight is fought,
   When the true deed is done —
Aloft in heaven's pure light,
(Deep azure crossed on white)
Our fair Church-Pennant waves
O'er a thousand thankful braves,
   Bareheaded in God's bright sun.

Lord of mercy and frown,
Ruling o'er sea and shore,
Send us such scene once more !
All in Line of Battle
When the black ships bear down
On tyrant fort and town,
Mid cannon cloud and rattle —
And the great guns once more
Thunder back the roar
Of the traitor walls ashore,
And the traitor flags come down !

Flag Ship Hartford, March, 1864.

ANNUS MEMORABILIS.

(CONGRESS, 1860-61.)

STAND strong and calm as Fate ! not a breath
of scorn or hate —
  Of taunt for the base, or of menace for the
    strong —
Since our fortunes must be sealed on that old and
    famous Field,
  Where the Right is set in battle with the Wrong.

'Tis coming, with the loom of Khamsin or Simoom,
  The tempest that shall try if we are of God or
    no —
Its roar is in the sky, — and they there be which cry,
  Let us cower, and the storm may over-blow.

Now, nay ! stand firm and fast ! (that was a spite-
    ful blast !)
  This is not a war of men, but of Angels Good
    and Ill —
'Tis hell that storms at heaven — 'tis the black
    and deadly Seven,
  Sworn 'gainst the Shining Ones to work their
    damnéd will !

How the Ether glooms and burns, as the tide of
     combat turns,
  And the smoke and dust above it whirl and float!
It eddies and it streams — and, certes, oft it seems
  As the Sins had the Seraphs fairly by the throat.

But we all have read, (in that Legend grand and
     dread,)
  How Michael and his host met the Serpent and
     his crew —
Naught has reached us of the Fight — but, if I have
     dreamed aright,
  'Twas a loud one and a long, as ever thundered
     through!

Right stiffly, past a doubt, the Dragon fought it
     out,
  And his Angels, each and all, did for Tophet
     their devoir —
There was creak of iron wings, and whirl of scor-
     pion stings,
  Hiss of bifid tongues, and the Pit in full uproar!

But, naught thereof enscrolled, in one brief line
     'tis told,
  (Calm as dew the Apocalyptic Pen,)
That on the Infinite Shore their place was found
     no more.
  God send the like on this our earth! Amen.

January 6th, 1861.

THE BATTLE SUMMERS.

AGAIN the glory of the days !
   Once more the dreamy sunshine fills
   Noon after noon, — and all the hills
Lie soft and dim in autumn haze.

And lovely lie these meadows low
   In the slant sun — and quiet broods
   Above the splendor of the woods
All touched with autumn's tenderest glow.

The trees stand marshalled, clan by clan,
   A bannered army, far and near —
   (Mark how yon fiery maples rear
Their crimson colors in the van !)

Methinks, these ancient haunts among,
   A fuller life informs the fall —
   The crows in council sit and call,
The quail through stubble leads her young.

The woodcock whirrs by bush and brake,
  The partridge plies his cedar-search —
  (Old Andy says the trout and perch
Are larger now, in stream and lake.)

O'er the brown leaves, the forest floor,
  With nut and acorn scantly strewed,
  The small red people of the wood
Are out to seek their winter store.

To-day they gather, each and all,
  To take their last of autumn suns —
  E'en the gray squirrel lithely runs
Along the mossy pasture wall.

By marsh and brook, by copse and hill,
  To their old quiet haunts repair
  The feeble things of earth and air,
And feed and flutter at their will.

The feet that roved this woodland round,
  The hands that scared the timid race,
  Now mingle in a mightier chase,
Or mould on that great Hunting-Ground.

Strange calm and peace! — ah, who could deem,
  By this still glen, this lone hill-side,
  How three long summers, in their pride,
Have smiled above that awful Dream? —

Have ever woven a braver green,
   And ever arched a lovelier blue ;
   Yet Nature, in her every hue,
Took color from the dread Unseen.

The haze of Indian Summer seemed
   Borne from far fields of sulphury breath —
   A subtile atmosphere of death
Was ever round us as we dreamed.

The horizon's dim heat-lightning played
   Like small-arms, still, thro' nights of drouth,
   And the low thunder of the south
Was dull and distant cannonade.

To us the glory or the gray
   Had still a stranger, stormier dye,
   Remembering how we watched the sky
Of many a waning battle day,

O'er many a field of loss or fame :
   How Shiloh's eve to ashes turned,
   And how Manassas' sunset burned
Incarnadine of blood and flame.

And how, in thunder, day by day,
   The hot sky hanging over all,
   Beneath that sullen, lurid pall,
The Week of Battles rolled away !

"Give me my legions!"—so, in grief,
  Like him of Rome, our Father cried:
  (A Nation's Flower lay down and died
In yon fell shade!)—ah, hapless chief—

Too late we learned thy star!—o'erta'en,
  (Of error or of fate o'erharsh,)
  Like Varus, in the fatal marsh
Where skill and valor all were vain!

All vain—Fair Oaks and Seven Pines!
  A deeper hue than dying Fall
  May lend, is yours!——yet over all
The mild Virginian autumn shines.

And still a Nation's Heart o'erhung
  The iron echoes pealed afar,
  Along a thousand leagues of war
The battle thunders tossed and flung.

Till, when our fortunes paled the most,
  And Hope had half forgot to wave
  Her banner o'er the wearied brave—
A morning saw the traitor host

Rolled back o'er red Potomac's wave.
  And the Great River burst his way!—
  And all on that dear Summer's Day,
Day that our fathers died and gave.

Rest in thy calm, Eternal Right !
   For thee, though levin-scarred and torn,
   Through flame and death shall still be borne
The Red, the Azure, and the White.

We pass — we sink like summer's snow —
   Yet on the mighty Cause shall move,
   Though every field a Cannæ prove,
And every pass a Roncesvaux.

Though every summer burn anew
   A battle-summer, — though each day
   We name a new Aceldema,
Or some dry Golgotha re-dew.

And thou, in lonely dream withdrawn !
   What dost thou, while in tempest dies
   The long drear Night, and all the skies
Are red with Freedom's fiery Dawn !

Behold, thy summer days are o'er —
   Yet dearer, lovelier these that fall
   Wrapped in red autumn's flag, than all
The green and glory gone before.

'Twas well to sing by stream and sod,
   And they there were that loved thy lays —
   But lo, where, 'neath yon battle-haze,
Thy brothers bare the breast for God !

Reck not of waning force nor breath —
   Some little aid may yet be thine,
   Some honor to the All-Divine, —
To-day, where, by yon River of Death,[4]

His stars on Rosecrans look down —
   Or, on the morrow, by moat and wall,
   Once more when the Great Admiral
Thunders on traitor fleet and town.

O wearied heart! O darkening eye!
   (How long to hope and trust untrue!)
   What in the hurly can ye do?
Little, 'tis like — yet we can die.

October, 1863.

SUSPIRIA ENSIS.

MOURN no more for our dead,
  Laid in their rest serene —
With the tears a Land hath shed
  Their graves shall ever be green.

Ever their fair, true glory
  Fondly shall fame rehearse —
Light of legend and story,
  Flower of marble and verse!

(Wilt thou forget, O Mother!
  How thy darlings, day by day,
For thee, and with fearless faces,
  Journeyed the darksome way —
Went down to death in the war-ship,
  And on the bare hill-side lay ?)

For the Giver they gave their breath,
  And 'tis now no time to mourn —
Lo, of their dear, brave death
  A mighty Nation is born!

But a long lament for others,
   Dying for Darker Powers!—
Those that once were our brothers,
   Whose children shall yet be ours.

That a People, haughty and brave,
   (Warriors, old and young!)
Should lie in a bloody grave,
   And never a dirge be sung!

We may look with woe on the dead,
   We may smooth their lids, 'tis true,
For the veins of a common red
   And the Mother's milk we drew.

But alas, how vainly bleeds
   The breast that is bared for Crime—
Who shall dare hymn the deeds
   That else had been all sublime?

Were it alien steel that clashed,
   They had guarded each inch of sod—
But the angry valor dashed
   On the awful shield of God!

(Ah—if for some great Good—
   On some giant Evil hurled—
The Thirty Millions had stood
   'Gainst the might of a banded world!)

But now, to the long, long Night
   They pass, as they ne'er had been —
A stranger and sadder sight
   Than ever the sun hath seen.

For his waning beams illume
   A vast and a sullen train
Going down to the gloom —
   One wretched and drear refrain
The only line on their tomb, —
   " They died — and they died in vain ! "

Gone — ay me ! — to the grave,
   And never one note of song —
The Muse would weep for the brave,
   But how shall she chant the wrong?

For a wayward Wench is she —
   One that rather would wait
With Old John Brown at the tree
   Than Stonewall dying in state.

When, for the wrongs that were,
   Hath she lilted a single stave?
Know, proud hearts, that, with her,
   'Tis not enough to be brave.

By the injured, with loving glance,
   Aye hath she lingered of old,
And eyed the Evil askance,
   Be it never so haught and bold.

With Homer, alms-gift in hand,
　With Dante, exile and free,
With Milton, blind in the Strand,
　With Hugo, lone by the sea !

In the attic, with Berangér,
　She could carol, how blithe and free !
Of the old, worn Frocks of Blue,
　(All threadbare with victory !) [5]
But never of purple and gold,
　Never of Lily or Bee !

And thus, though the Traitor Sword
　Were the bravest that battle wields —
Though the fiery Valor poured
　Its life on a thousand fields —

The sheen of its ill renown
　All tarnished with guilt and blame,
No Poet a deed may crown,
　No Lay may laurel a name.

Yet never for thee, fair Song !
　The fallen brave to condemn ;
They died for a mighty Wrong —
　But their Demon died with them.

(Died, by field and by city !) —
　Be thine on the day to dwell,
When dews of peace and of pity
　Shall fall o'er the fading hell —

And the dead shall smile in Heaven —
And tears, that now may not rise,
Of love and of all forgiveness,
Shall stream from a million eyes.

Flag Ship Hartford, at Sea,
January, 1864.

DOWN!

(APRIL, 1865.)

YARD-ARM to yard-arm we lie
Alongside the Ship of Hell —
And still through the sulphury sky
The terrible clang goes high,
Broadside and battle cry,
And the pirates' maddened yell!

Our Captain's cold on the deck,
Our brave Lieutenant's a wreck —
He lies in the hold there, hearing
The storm of fight going on overhead,
Tramp and thunder to wake the dead!
The great guns jumping overhead,
And the whole ship's company cheering!

Four hours the Death-Fight has roared,
    (Gun-deck and berth-deck blood-wet!)
Her mainmast's gone by the board,
Down come topsail and jib!
We're smashing her, rib by rib,
And the pirate yells grow weak —
    But the Black Flag flies there yet,
The Death's Head grinning a-peak!

Long has she haunted the seas,
Terror of sun and breeze!
Her deck has echoed with groans,
    Her hold is a horrid den
Piled to the orlop with bones
    Of starved and of murdered men —
They swarm 'mid her shrouds in hosts,
The smoke is murky with ghosts!

But to-day, her cruise shall be short —
She's bound to the Port she cleared from,
She's nearing the Light she steered from —
    Ah, the Horror sees her fate!
Heeling heavy to port,
    She strikes, but all too late!
Down, with her curséd crew,
    Down, with her damnéd freight,
To the bottom of the Blue,
Ten thousand fathom deep!
    With God's glad sun o'erhead —
That is the way to weep,
    So will we mourn our dead!

WORDS THAT CAN BE SUNG

OLD John Brown lies a-mouldering in the
grave,
Old John Brown lies slumbering in his grave —
But John Brown's soul is marching with the brave,
His soul is marching on.
Glory, glory, hallelujah!
Glory, glory, hallelujah!
Glory, glory, hallelujah!
His soul is marching on.

He has gone to be a soldier in the Army of the
Lord,
He is sworn as a private in the ranks of the
Lord —
He shall stand at Armageddon with his brave old
sword,
When Heaven is marching on.
Glory, etc.
For Heaven is marching on.

3   D

He shall file in front where the lines of battle form,
He shall face to front when the squares of battle
       form —
Time with the column, and charge in the storm,
              Where men are marching on.
         Glory, etc.
             True men are marching on.

Ah, foul tyrants! do ye hear him where he comes?
Ah, black traitors! do ye know him as he comes?
In thunder of the cannon and roll of the drums,
             As we go marching on.
         Glory, etc.
             We all are marching on.

Men may die, and moulder in the dust —
Men may die, and arise again from dust,
Shoulder to shoulder, in the ranks of the Just,
            When Heaven is marching on.
         Glory, etc.
            The Lord is marching on.

April 17th, 1862.

THE EAGLE OF CORINTH.[6]

DID you hear of the Fight at Corinth,
     How we whipped out Price and Van Dorn?
Ah, that day we earned our rations —
(Our cause was God's and the Nation's,
     Or we'd have come out forlorn!)
A long and a terrible day!
And, at last, when night grew gray,
By the hundred, there they lay,
(Heavy sleepers, you'd say,)
     That wouldn't wake on the morn.

Our staff was bare of a flag,
We didn't carry a rag
     In those brave marching days —
Ah, no — but a finer thing!
With never a cord or string,
An Eagle, of ruffled wing,
     And an eye of awful gaze!

The grape it rattled like hail,
The minies were dropping like rain,

The first of a thunder-shower —
  The wads were blowing like chaff,
(There was pounding, like floor and flail,
 All the front of our line!)
So we stood it, hour after hour —
 But our eagle, he felt fine!
  'Twould have made you cheer and laugh,
To see, through that iron gale,
How the Old Fellow'd swoop and sail
Above the racket and roar —
To right and to left he'd soar,
But ever came back, without fail,
  And perched on his standard-staff.

All that day, I tell you true,
 They had pressed us, steady and fair,
 Till we fought in street and square —
(The affair, you might think, looked blue,)
 But we knew we had them there!
Our works and batteries were few,
Every gun, they'd have sworn, they knew —
But, you see, there was one or two
 We had fixed for them, unaware.

 They reckon they've got us now!
  For the next half hour 'twill be warm —
Aye, aye, look yonder! — I vow,
If they weren't Secesh, how I'd love them!
  Only see how grandly they form,
(Our eagle whirling above them,)
  To take Robinett by storm!

They're timing ! — it can't be long —
Now for the nub of the fight !
    (You may guess that we held our breath,)
By the Lord, 'tis a splendid sight !
  A column two thousand strong
    Marching square to the death !

On they came, in solid column,
  For once, no whooping nor yell —
(Ah, I dare say they felt solemn.)
    Front and flank — grape and shell —
      Our batteries pounded away !
And the minies hummed to remind 'em
      They had started on no child's play !
  Steady they kept a-going,
But a grim wake settled behind 'em —
  From the edge of the *abattis*,
      (Where our dead and dying lay
  Under fence and fallen tree,)
      Up to Robinett, all the way
The dreadful swath kept growing !
      'Twas butternut, flecked with gray.

Now for it, at Robinett !
Muzzle to muzzle, we met —
  (Not a breath of bluster or brag,
    Not a lisp for quarter or favor) —
Three times, there, by Robinett,
With a rush, their feet they set
On the logs of our parapet,

And waved their bit of a flag —
    What could be finer or braver !
But our cross-fire stunned them in flank,
They melted, rank after rank —
(O'er them, with terrible poise,
   Our Bird did circle and wheel !)
      Their whole line began to waver —
Now for the bayonet, boys !
   On them with the cold steel !

Ah, well — you know how it ended —
    We did for them, there and then,
  But their pluck, throughout, was splendid.
(As I said before, I could love them !)
     They stood, to the last, like men —
Only a handful of them
    Found the way back again.
   Red as blood, o'er the town,
   The angry sun went down,
     Firing flagstaff and vane —
And our eagle, — as for him,
There, all ruffled and grim,
    He sat, o'erlooking the slain !

Next morning, you'd have wondered
    How we had to drive the spade !
  There, in great trenches and holes,
  (Ah, God rest their poor souls !)
We piled some fifteen hundred,
    Where that last charge was made !

Sad enough, I must say.
　No mother to mourn and search,
No priest to bless or to pray —
We buried them where they lay,
　Without a rite of the church —
But our eagle, all that day,
　Stood solemn and still on his perch.

'Tis many a stormy day
　Since, out of the cold, bleak North,
　Our great War-Eagle sailed forth
To swoop o'er battle and fray.
Many and many a day
　O'er charge and storm hath he wheeled,
　Foray and foughten field,
　　　Tramp, and volley, and rattle ! —
　Over crimson trench and turf,
　Over climbing clouds of surf,
Through tempest and cannon-rack,
　Have his terrible pinions whirled —
　　　(A thousand fields of battle !
　　　A million leagues of foam !)
But our Bird shall yet come back,
　　　He shall soar to his Eyrie-Home —
　And his thundrous wings be furled,
　In the gaze of a gladdened world,
　　　On the Nation's loftiest Dome.

December, 1862.

THE COLOR-BEARER.[1]

(VICKSBURG, MAY 22, 1863.)

LET them go! — they are brave, I know —
 But a berth like this, why it suits me best;
I can't carry back the Old Colors to-day,
We've come together a long, rough way —
 Here's as good a spot as any to rest.

No look, I reckon, to hold them long;
 So here, in the turf, with my bayonet,
To dig for a bit, and plant them strong —
 (Look out for the point — we may want it yet!)

Dry work! — but the old canteen holds fast
 A few drops of water — not over-fresh —
So, for a drink! — it may be the last —
 My respects to you, Mr. Secesh!

No great show for the snakes to sight;
 Our boys keep 'em busy yet, by the powers! —
Hark, what a row going on, to the Right!
 Better luck there, I hope, than ours.

Half an hour ! — (and you'd swear 'twas three) —
　　Here, by the bully old staff, I've sat —
Long enough, as it seems to me,
　　To lose as many lives as a cat.

Now and then, they sputter away ;
　　A puff and a crack, and I hear the ball.
Mighty poor shooting, I should say —
　　Not bad fellows, may be, after all.

My chance, of course, isn't worth a dime —
　　But I thought 'twould be over, sudden and quick
Well, since it seems that we're not on time,
　　Here's for a touch of the Kilikinick.

Cool as a clock ! — and, what is strange,
　　Out of this dream of death and alarm,
(This wild, hard week of battle and change,)
Out of the rifle's deadly range —
　　My thoughts are all at the dear old farm.

'Tis green as a sward, by this, I know —
　　The orchard is just beginning to set,
They mowed the home-lot a week ago —
　　The corn must be late, for that piece is wet.

I can think of one or two, that would wipe
　　A drop or so from a soft blue eye,
To see me sit and puff at my pipe,
　　With a hundred death's heads grinning hard by.

3*

And I wonder, when this has all passed o'er,
   And the tattered old stars in triumph wave on
Through street and square, with welcoming roar,
   If ever they'll think of us who are gone?

How we marched together, sound or sick,
   Sank in the trench o'er the heavy spade —
How we charged on the guns, at double-quick,
Kept rank for Death to choose and to pick —
   And lay on the bed no fair hands made.

Ah, well! — at last, when the Nation's free,
   And flags are flapping from bluff to bay,
In old St. Lou what a time there'll be!
I mayn't be there, the Hurrah to see —
   But if the Old Rag goes back to-day,
They never shall say 'twas carried by me!

A WAR STUDY.

METHINKS, all idly and too well
 We love this Nature — little care
  (Whate'er her children brave and bear,)
Were hers, though any grief befell.

With gayer sunshine still she seeks
 To gild our trouble, so 'twould seem ;
  Through all this long, tremendous Dream,
A tear hath never wet her cheeks.

And such a scene I call to mind —
 The third day's thunder, (fort and fleet,
  And the great guns beneath our feet,)
Was dying, and a warm gulf wind

Made monotone 'mid stays and shrouds :
 O'er books and men in quiet chat
  With the Great Admiral I sat,
Watching the lovely cannon-clouds.

For still, from mortar and from gun,
 Or short-fused shell that burst aloft,
  Outsprung a rose-wreath, bright and soft,
Tinged with the redly setting sun.

And I their beauty praised : but he,
  The grand old Senior, strong and mild,
  (Of head a sage, in heart a child,)
Sighed for the wreck that still must be.

Flag Ship Hartford, March, 1864.

BURY THEM.

(WAGNER, JULY 18, 1863.)

BURY the Dragon's Teeth !
  Bury them deep and dark ! '
  The incisors swart and stark,
  The molars heavy and dark —
And the one white Fang underneath !

Bury the Hope Forlorn !
  Never shudder to fling,
With its fellows dusky and worn,
  The strong and beautiful thing,
  (Pallid ivory and pearl !)
  Into the horrible Pit —
Hurry it in, and hurl
  All the rest over it !

Trample them, clod by clod,
   Stamp them in dust amain !
  The cuspids, cruent and red,
  That the Monster, Freedom, shed
On the sacred, strong Slave-Sod —
   They never shall rise again !

Never ? — what hideous growth
  Is sprouting through clod and clay ?
  What Terror starts to the day ?
A crop of steel, on our oath !
  How the burnished stamens glance ! —
Spike, and anther, and blade,
How they burst from the bloody shade,
  And spindle to spear and lance !

There are tassels of blood-red maize —
  How the horrible Harvest grows !
'Tis sabres that glint and daze —
'Tis bayonets all ablaze
  Uprearing in dreadful rows !

For one that we buried there,
A thousand are come to air !
Ever, by door-stone and hearth,
They break from the angry earth —
  And out of the crimson sand,
Where the cold white Fang was laid,
Rises a terrible Shade,
  The Wraith of a sleepless Brand !

And our hearts wax strange and chill,
With an ominous shudder and thrill,
   Even here, on the strong Slave-Sod,
Lest, haply, we be found,
(Ah, dread no brave hath drowned !)
   Fighting against Great God.

WOOD AND COAL.

(November, 1863.)

FARMER SMITH shakes his old white head,
   Fuel, he says, will be scarce and dear —
Half our young men are gone to the wars,
   Little wood has been cut this year.

Skipper Jones strokes his grizzled beard,
   Freights, he expects, were never so high —
Half our hands are shipped on the fleets,
   Coals must be awful, by and by !

Are ye glad, O Cedar and Fir ?
   Will ye sing, with the Seer of yore,
Rejoice ! no feller, axe in hand,
   Cometh against us more !

Hush, with your wavy boast,
　Your flutter of leafy words !
　The funeral train of your Lords
Goes down from mountain to coast.

Their dirge is strident and hoarse —
　Screech of bob-sled and chain,
　Groan of drag and of wain,
Reeling under the giant corse
Of Oak from Merrimac's rugged source
　And Pine from the hills of Maine.

And down where the dock-yard sits,
　With mighty derrick and sheers —
Keel and carline, transom and bitts,
The mammoth Skeleton grows, and knits
　*The spoil of your hundred years.

Are ye quiet, Kobold and Gnome ?
　Can ye crouch and whisper at will,
By lode and drift, in your sullen home,
　Untroubled with pick or drill ?

Hark, how angry and fast,
　By valley and mountain-gorge,
By port and foundry vast,
The roar of furnace and blast,
　The clang of anvil and forge !

For the Powers of Earth to-day
  Are sounding an old, old Song —
The loud and the dreadful Lay
  Of death to horror and wrong!

A thousand years hath it rang,
  "Crime shall go under!"
Is all but a vast, vain pang?
  God makes no blunder —
How the armories bellow and clang!
  How the ship-yards thunder!

———————

Ah, not for the fireside glow,
  With its cheery urn and tray,
And the children's faces all a-row,
  Are the woods and the mines, to-day!

  Scant is the spark ye spare for these,
  Dark-ledged caverns and moss-gray trees!
A grimmer service is yours at last —
To roll the plate and to melt the cast,
Bolt the keelson and step the mast,
  And drive the war-ship through winter seas.

So hath it been from the days of old —
  Though the fire go out on the widow's hearth,
And the orphans cuddle abed for cold —
  That is the way of our weary earth,
  These are the pangs of a Nation's Birth.

Trust and endure! — for 'tis all of Fate —
And the end shall come, be it soon or late —
   Better that one generation die,
Than a hundred live in horror and hate —
   There's room for us all in God's fair sky.

NIGHT-QUARTERS.

TANG! tang! went the gong's wild roar
   Through the hundred cells of our great Sea-
     Hive!
Five seconds — it couldn't be more —
And the whole Swarm was humming and alive —
   (We were on an enemy's shore).

   With savage haste, in the dark,
   (Our steerage hadn't a spark,)
  Into boot and hose they blundered —
From for'ard came a strange, low roar,
   The dull and smothered racket
   Of lower rig and jacket
  Hurried on, by the hundred —
How the berth deck buzzed and swore!

The third of minutes ten,
And half a thousand men,
From the dream-gulf, dead and deep,
Of the seaman's measured sleep,
In the taking of a lunar,
    In the serving of a ration,
    Every man at his station ! —
Three and a quarter, or sooner !
    Never a skulk to be seen —
From the look-out aloft to the gunner
    Lurking in his black magazine.

There they stand, still as death,
And, (a trifle out of breath,
    It may be,) we of the Staff,
All on the poop, to a minute,
Wonder if there's anything in it —
    Doubting if to growl or laugh.

    But, somehow, every hand
    Feels for hilt and brand,
Tries if buckle and frog be tight —
    So, in the chilly breeze, we stand
Peering through the dimness of the night —
    The men, by twos and ones,
    Grim and silent at the guns,
Ready, if a Foe heave in sight !

But, as we looked aloft,
There, all white and soft,

Floated on the fleecy clouds,
(Stray flocks in heaven's blue croft) —
How they shone, the eternal stars,
'Mid the black masts and spars
    And the great maze of lifts and shrouds !

Flag Ship Hartford, May, 1864.

COMING.

(APRIL, 1861.)

WORLD, art thou 'ware of a storm ?
    Hark to the ominous sound,
How the far-off gales their battle form,
    And the great sea swells feel ground !

It comes, the Typhoon of Death —
    Near and nearer it comes !
The horizon thunder of cannon-breath
    And the roar of angry drums !

Hurtle, Terror sublime !
    Swoop o'er the Land, to-day —
So the mist of wrong and crime,
The breath of our Evil Time,
    Be swept, as by fire, away !

SUMTER.

SO, they *will* have it!
  The Black Witch, (curse on her,)
    Always had won her
Greediest demand — for we gave it —
    All but our honor!

Thirty hours thundered
    Siege-guns and mortars —
    (Flames in the quarters!)
One to a hundred
    Stood our brave Forters!

No more of parties! —
    Let them all moulder —
    Here's work that's bolder!
Forward, my hearties!
    Shoulder to shoulder.

Sight o'er the trunnion —
    Send home the rammer —
    Linstock and hammer!
Speak for the Union!
    Tones that won't stammer!

Men of Columbia,
  Leal hearts from Annan,
  Brave lads of Shannon !
We are all one to-day —
  On with the cannon !

APRIL 19, 1775 – 1861.

ONCE again, (our dear old Massachusetts !)
  Once again the drops that made their way,
Red, ah not in vain ! on that old greensward —
  It is six and eighty years this very day.

Six and eighty years — aye, it seemed but a mem-
    ory —
  Little left of all that glory — so we thought —
Only the old firelocks hung on farm-house chim-
    neys,
  And rude blades the village blacksmith wrought.

Only here and there a white head that remembers
  How the Frocks of Homespun stood against
    King George —
How the hard hands stretched them o'er the scanty
    embers
  When the sleet and snow came down at Valley
    Forge.

Once more, dear Brother-State ! thy pure, brave
    blood baptizes
  Our last and noblest struggle for freedom and
    for right —
It fell on the cruel stones ! — but an awful Nation
    rises
  In the glory of its conscience, and the splendor
    of its might.

April 19th, 1861.

ON FIRE.

" THE furnace is kindling," Mohammed said,
   As he stood on El Honein's height —
Through the black defile began to spread
Clink and glimmer, angry and red,
  Of the fiery spears in fight.

Our spark is stricken ! — how fast
  The mighty furnace hath lit !
Or ever an hour be past,
'Twill roar, the terrible Blast,
  Roar and seethe like the Pit !

Aye, many the day it hath
  Stood, heaped with fuel o'ermuch —

Horrors piled for the flame's red path,
Wrath laid up for the Day of Wrath,
　　And Wrong, with its tinder touch.

And, to-day, 'tis fairly ablaze —
　　Listen, ye that have laughed!
Hark, in stolid amaze,
'Mid the crackle of hate and craze,
　　To the low, dull roar of the draught!

It sparkles savage and dire!
　　The forky tongues flicker lithe —
How they grapple, faster and higher,
The greedy serpents of fire,
　　And the candent scales, how they writhe!

The Furnace kindles! what hand shall tame
　　Its rage, till it roar at height?
Grant, O God, that from out the same,
The whirl and fury, the heat and shame —
Thy fierce Alembic of blood and flame —
　　A Nation's Soul come white.

LET US ALONE.

"All we aṡk is to be let alone."

A S vonce I valked by a dismal svamp,
   There sot an Old Cove in the dark and damp,
And at everybody as passed that road
A stick or a stone this Old Cove throwed.
And venever he flung his stick or his stone,
He'd set up a song of "Let me alone."

"Let me alone, for I loves to shy
These bits of things at the passers by —
Let me alone, for I've got your tin
And lots of other traps snugly in —
Let me alone, I'm riggin' a boat
To grab votever you've got afloat —
In a veek or so I expects to come
And turn you out of your 'ouse and 'ome —
I'm a quiet Old Cove," says he, vith a groan :
"All I axes is — Let me alone."

Just then came along, on the self-same vay,
Another Old Cove, and began for to say —
"Let you alone ! That's comin' it strong ! —
You've *ben* let alone — a darned sight too long —

Of all the sarce that ever I heerd !
Put down that stick ! (You may well look skeered.)
Let go that stone ! If you once show fight,
I'll knock you higher than ary kite.
You must hev a lesson to stop your tricks,
And cure you of shying them stones and sticks —
And I'll hev my hardware back and my cash,
And knock your scow into tarnal smash ;
And if ever I catches you round my ranch,
I'll string you up to the nearest branch.
The best you can do is to go to bed,
And keep a decent tongue in your head ;
For I reckon, before you and I are done,
You'll wish you had let honest folks alone."

The Old Cove stopped, and the t'other Old Cove
He sot quite still in his cypress grove,
And he looked at his stick, revolvin' slow
Vether 'twere safe to shy it or no —
And he grumbled on, in an injured tone,
" All that I axed vos, *let me alone.*"

THE MARCH OF THE REGIMENT.

HERE they come! — 'tis the Twelfth, you
    know —
  The Colonel is just at hand —
The ranks close up, to the measured flow
  Of music cheery and grand.
Glitter on glitter, row by row,
The steady bayonets, on they go
  For God and the Right to stand —
Another Thousand to front the Foe!
And to die — if it must be even so —
  For the dear old Fatherland!

O, trusty and true! O gay, warm heart!
  O, manly and earnest brow!
Here, in the hurrying street, we part —
  To meet — ah, where and how?
O, ready and staunch! who, at war's alarm,
On lonely hill-side and mountain-farm
  Have left the axe and the plow!
That every tear were a holy charm,
To guard, with honor, some head from harm,
  And to quit some generous vow!

For, of valiant heart and of sturdy arm
　　Was never more need than now.

Never a nobler Morn to the bold
　　For God and for Country's sake !
Lo, a Flag, so haughtly unrolled
On a hundred foughten fields of old,
　　Now flaunts in a pirate's wake !
The Lion coys in each blazoned fold,
　　And leers on the blood-barred Snake !

O, base and vain ! that, for grudge and gain,
　　Could a century's feud renew —
Could hoard your hate for the coward chance
When a Nation reeled in a wilder Dance
　　Of Death, than the Switzer drew !
We have borne, and borne — and may bear again
　　With wrong, but if wrong from *you*,

Welcome, the sulphury cloud in the sky !
　　Welcome, the crimson rain !
Act but the dream ye dared to form,
Strike a single spark ! — and the storm
Of serried bayonets sweeping by,
　　Shall swell to a hurricane !

Dree your weird ! — though an hour may blight,
　　In treason, a century's fame —
Trust Greed and Spite ! — (sith Reason and Right
　　Lie cold, with Honor and Shame) —

And learn anon — as on that dread night
When, the dead around and the deck aflame,
From John Paul's lip the fierce word came —
   "We have only *begun* to fight!"

O, blind and bitter! that could not know,
Even in fight, a caitiff blow,
(Foully dealt on a hard-set foe,)
   Ever is underwise —
Ever is ghosted with after Fear —
Ye might lesson it — year by year,
   Looking, with fevered eyes,
For sail or smoke from the Breton shore,
Lest a Land, so rudely wronged of yore,
   In flamy revenge should rise!

Office at outcry! — ah, wretched Flam!
   Vile Farce of hammer and prate!
Trade! bids Derby — and blood! smirks Pam —
Little ween they, each courtly Sham,
   Of the Terror lying in wait!
Little wot of the web he spins,
Their Tempter in purple, that darkly grins
   'Neath his stony visor of state,
O'er Seas, how narrow! — for, whoso wins,
At yon base Auction of Outs and Ins,
   The rule of his Dearest Hate —
Her point once flashing athwart her Kin's,
And the reckoning, ledgered for long, begins —
The galling Glories and envied Sins
   Shall buzz in a mesh like fate!

Aye, mate your meanest ! — ye can but do
That permitted — when Heaven would view
How wrong, self-branded, her rage must rue
In wreck and ashes ! — (such scene as you,
    If wise, shall witness afar) —
How Guilt, o'erblown, her crest heaves high,
And dares the injured, with taunt, to try
    Ordeal of Fire in war —
Blindfold and brazen, on God doth call —
Then grasps, in horror, the glaring ball,
    Or treads on the candent bar !

Yet a little ! — and men shall mark
This our Moloch, who sate so stark,
(These hundred winters through godless dark
    Grinning o'er death and shame) —
Marking for murder each unbowed head,
Throned on his Ghizeh of bones, and fed
Still with hearts of the holy dead —
Naught but a Spectre foul and dread,
    Naught but a hideous Name !
At last ! — (ungloom, stern coffined frown !
Rest thee, Gray-Steel ! — aye, dead Renown !
In flame and thunder by field and town
The Giant-Horror is going down,
    Down to the Home whence it came !)

Deaf to the Doom that waits the Beast,
Still would ye share the Harlot's Feast,
    And drink of her blood-grimed Cup !

Pause ! — the Accursèd, on yon frenzied shore,
Buyeth your merchandise never more !
Mark, 'mid the Fiery Dew that drips,
Redder, faster, through black Eclipse,
How Sodom, to-night, shall sup !
(Thus the Kings, in Apocalypse,
The traders of souls and crews of ships,
Standing afar, with pallid lips,
While Babylon's Smoke goes up !)

Aye, 'tis at hand ! — foul lips, be dumb !
Our Armageddon is yet to come !
But cheery bugle, and angry drum,
With volleyed rattle and roar,
And cannon thunder-throb, shall be drowned,
That day, in a grander, stormier sound —
The Land, from mountain to shore,
Hurling shackle and scourge and stake
Back to their Lender of pit and lake —
('Twas Tophet leased them of yore) —
Hell, in her murkiest hold, shall quake,
As they ring on the damnèd floor !
O mighty Heart ! thou wast long to wake —
'Tis thine, to-morrow, to win or break
In a deadlier close once more —
If but for the dear and glorious sake
Of those who have gone before.

O Fair and Faithful ! that, sun by sun,
Slept on the field, or lost or won —

Children dear of the Holy One!
  Rest in your wintry sod.
Rest, your noble Devoir is done —
Done — and forever! — ours, to-day,
The dreary drift and the frozen clay
  By trampling armies trod —
The smoky shroud of the War-Simoom,
The maddened Crime at bay with her Doom,
  And fighting it, clod by clod.
O Calm and Glory! — beyond the gloom,
Above the bayonets bend and bloom
  The lilies and palms of God.

February, 1862.

LINES

BY OUR CORPORAL.

H A, boys! what's that we hear
    Out of the South so clear?
Cannon and thunder-cheer,
      True hearts and loyal! —
Aye, 'tis Dupont at work,
Shelling the snakes that lurk
      Down by Port Royal!

What's this from old Kentuck?
There, down upon his luck,
   Puts many a flying scamp
      What could you offer
To stop him as he scuds?
Not all the baby duds [8]
   Hived in your thieving camp,
      Black Zollicoffer!

Straight through Tennessee
The flag is flapping free —
      Aye, nothing shorter!
But first, with shot and shell,
The road was cleared right well —
Ye made each muzzle tell,
      Brave Foote and Porter!

Shear the old Stripes and Stars
Short, for the Bloody Bars?
      No —— not an atom!
How, 'neath yon cannon-smoke,
Volley and charge and stroke,
Roar around Roanoke! —
      Burnside is at 'em!

O, brave lads of the West,
Joy to each valiant breast!
Three days of steady fight —
Three shades of stormy night —
      Donelson tumbles.
Surrender, out of hand!

"Unchivalrous demand!"
    (So Buckner grumbles.)

March in, stout Grant and Smith,
(Ah, souls of pluck and pith!)
Haul down, for the Old Flag,
That black and bloody rag —
Twelve thousand in a bag!
    True hearts are overjoyed —
But half as many scamper,
(Ah, there's the only damper!)
Through the very worst of weathers,
After old Fuss-and-Feathers
    And foul Barabbas-Floyd.

Was't funk that made them flee?
Nay — they're as bold as we —
'Twas their bad cause, d'ye see,
Whereof they well were knowing,
(For all their brag and blowing,
Their cursing and their crowing,)
    That is what cowed 'em!
Keep the Old Flag a-going —
    Crowd 'em, boys, crowd 'em!

No more palaver!
  Speeches ain't glory —
  Sink whig and tory!
Rifle clean, bayonet keen,
Saddle tight, sabre bright,
  These tell the story!

4*

HEARTS OF OAK. — AN EPITAPH.

(MARCH 8, 1862.)

TO quarters — stand by, my hearties !
  Every shot to-day must tell —
Here they come at last, the lubbers,
  Boxed up in their iron shell.

Aye, she's heading dead athwart us,
  Where the fog begins to lift —
Now a broadside, and all together,
  At the bloody rope-walk adrift !

How the hog-back's snout comes on us !
  Give it again to 'em, boys !
Ah, there 's a crash at our counter
  Can be heard through all the noise !

'Tis like pitching of peas and pebbles —
  No matter for that, my men,
Stand by, to send 'em another —
  Ah, I think we hulled her then !

Carpenter, how is the water?
    Gaining, sir, faster and higher;
'Tis all awash in the ward-room —
    Never mind — we can load and fire !

Let them charge with their Iron Devil,
    They never shall see our backs —
What, all afloat on our gun-deck ?
    Aye, your sponges and rammers to the racks !

Sinking, my hearts, at an anchor —
    But never say die till it's o'er !
Are you ready there on the spar-deck ?
    We'll give them one round more.

Ready all, on the spar-deck !
    Aye, my lads, we're going down —
She's heeling — but one more broadside
    For the Navy and its old renown !
Hurrah ! there go the splinters !
    Ha, they shall know us where we drown !

Now one cheer more, my hearties,
    For the Flag and its brave renown !
They shall hear it, the fine old captains,
    With Hull and Perry looking down.

They're watching us, where we founder,
    With a tear on each tough old cheek —
Down she goes, our noble frigate,
    But the Old Flag's still at her peak !

It waves o'er the blood-red water —
   Lawrence sees it where it flies !
And they look down, our grand old captains,
  · With a tear and a smile from the skies.

ON THE KILLING OF CERTAIN DOGS.[9]

A YE, we'll block that game — or try to !
      There's more of 'em down this way —
Uncle, are yonder the kennels ?
   Yes, mas'r — sorry to say.

Sure enough — hark, what a baying !
   A heap of 'em, I'll be bound.
Here's one coming to meet us —
   Boys, what a handsome hound !

My eyes — such wagging and leaping !
   So jolly, you'd never think
He could tree and watch a white human,
   Or tear his throat, at a wink !

Poor fellow — so pleased to be petted !
   Little knowing where it ends —
Seeing us with the old darkey,
   He fancies we are his friends.

No fault of thine, my doggie,
  (Poor honest beast of God!)
That devils taught thee to snuff the trail
  Where bleeding feet have trod.

But creatures, dumb or human,
  Good, it may be, at their birth,
Once trained in the school of Satan,
  Can be trusted no more on earth.

We know that 'tis no use trying
  To teach an old dog new tricks —
By Jove, I'd be glad to save him!
  But can't, anyway you can fix.

Here's for it, then! though it goes,
  I tell you, against the grain —
But it's right, and it must be done —
  He shan't feel a minute's pain.

'Tis but a click and a bound!
  And there he lies — poor old pup!
Boys! I'd rather be that dead hound
  Than the devil that brought him up.

MR. CARLYLE'S CHIMNEY,[10]

AND WHAT WOULD COME OF MEDDLING WITH IT.

'OORAH, neighbors! vot do yer say —
  'Ere's a chimney afire across the vay!
It 'asn't been burnt this many a day —
   And there can't be no manner of doubt
But the flues is choked vith soot and vith dirt —
Let's hall turn to, in veskit and shirt,
Vith 'and-pump and hengine, basin and squirt,
(Hanything as will swash or spirt)
   And see if we can't put it hout!

'Tis a heasy business, I'll be bail —
So form your line, vith bucket and pail,
   We know vot we're about!
The folks of the 'ouse, 'ow they scold and curse,
" Keep hoff! — you'll honly make matters vorse!
   It 'as got to burn itself hout!"
Never you mind! — let's come at the flue!
We're 'ere, and we're bound to put them through —
   Bear an 'and vith the spout!

Varm vork, gen'lemen! — faith, I see
'Tis more of a job than we took it to be —

('Urry up, vith yer 'ose !!)
For the more we pumps, and the 'arder we pours,
The faster it burns, and the louder it roars,
 And the 'otter and 'otter it grows !

'Ow the swash drips back, like scalding tears,
And the burning soot comes about our hears,
 And the flame 'owls 'igher and 'igher !
Look hout ! the mantle is catching ! (whew !
 For vun, I begins to tire) —
'Ullo ! by George, this never will do !
Ventre' bleu, mo'sieur ! and me tink so too —
 Ve sall 'ave ze 'ole str-r-r-eet avire !

And now, vot next ? we can do no more —
 Their hentries and stairvays is stamped vith
  mud,
 Their rugs and carpets soaked in a flood —
But the 'orrible Flue keeps on to roar —
Vot a dreadful puddle lies on the floor !
 By this blaze, you'd svear t'was blood !

THE FALL OF AL-ACCOUB.[1]

" And now, behold, the axe is laid unto the root of the tree."

KNOW ye the fall is nigh
    Of the dreadful Tree Al-Accoub?
He had thrust his top so high,
The Upas-breath floated by
Those who, in God's sweet sky,
    Sit with Isa and Yacoub.

Tree in whose ghastly shadow
    Never a green thing grew,
    Never a bright bud blew!
It hangs o'er a mighty meadow,
    Whose dreary Vast never knew
    One tear of heaven's sweet dew,
The blear and the blasted meadow —
    But dripping of venom-dew,
    Manzaneel's blister-dew.

Ha! how the Horror stands
Clutching, with monstrous hands,
    Hold on earth and on hell!
With the snaky shroud and stay

Of polypus-rigged Jaguéy,
    (Throats that flatten and swell !)
Massy buttress and knee
Shore up the terrible Tree,
    Spur, and elbow, and crook,
In savage rugæ and whelks,
(Like horns of the giant elks,) —
        Its roots lay hold on hell —
    They burrow, and gnarl, and hook
    At the wormiest heart of hell.

(Thus, in a strange, weird land —
    A far-off Isle of the South,
        Deep in the Gulfy Wave —
    There's a ledge by a jagged mouth,
        The upper jaw of a cave ;
            On the very brink of it
A mighty Ceiba doth stand,
        Spreading him broad and brave ;
            Huge, and writhing, and knit,
His roots show horribly grand —
Coil and cable and strand
        Stretching down to the Pit.)[12]

    Round him doth climb and fold
Full many a villainous thing.
    Freckled, and scaled, and rolled
In grisly spiral and ring,
They wind like boas, or cling
    With cruel centipede-hold ;

'Mid the Inner-Dark, untold,
    Ghastlier forms lie screened
Of Hates, and Terrors, and Pangs,
    (Anguish never was weened !)
Ah, the thorns are claws and fangs,
Every fruit thereon that hangs,
    The ashen mask of a fiend !

Vast is the Shadow across,
  Rarely the gaze may win,
(Save when the swamp-winds toss
The black witch-mantle of moss,) ·
  A glimpse of the gloom within —
Of the infinite Swarm of Shapes —
Myriads of wretched Shapes,
  That ever thereunder flit,
    Wraiths of Evil and Dread —
(Souls worn back to the ape's —
  Suicides — Ghouls that sit,
    All agrime, at their dead !)

Ever therefrom doth flow
The scent and the sound of woe,
  Out of its shroud of old
Steaming sullen and slow —
  Blight of fungus and mould,
    Taint of blood and of ordure —
Sobs that strangle and strive,
Groan as of gag and gyve,
Hum of a maddened Hive

Swarming for sting and torture —
The whole foul Mass is alive
With twining horror and torture!

Ha, how they coil and clasp!
They plicate, constrict, and gasp,
In plexure horribly writhen!
Knotting closer and madder —
Every bough is a python,
Every twig is an adder,
Every spray is an asp!

Ah, the puff and dilation!
The hiss, and the forked vibration
Darting fiercer and further!
The bloody cockatrice-wattle,
The horny pods that rattle —
Horrid crotalus-rattle!
Shrilling venom and murther.

Hollow its heart of old,
Yet grimly it keeps its hold —
So stark it stands and so bold,
Devil-dom deems 'tis sound —
Swears by it still, — though now
And then some rottener bough
Comes with a crash to ground.

For to-day 'tis stormy weather —
Night and tempest together
Swooping from East and North —

Thunder by sea and land !
The great Line-Gales are at hand —
    What may the morn bring forth ?

    Steady it comes and strong.
How, as the bulk is stirred,
The creak and the clang are heard
Of bat and of unclean bird,
    That lodged in its limbs so long —
        Screech, and flutter, and wail !
How, as the black winds rouse
The wrath of its savage boughs,
        It rocks and roars in the gale !

Vast and angry commotion !
Lift and thunder of ocean,
    Forest riving and roar —
        Trouble in earth and sky,
    Wreck by mountain and shore —
Terror and doom ! — is it *Thee*,
Thou black and blasphemous Tree !
        The Vengeance shall yet pass by ?

    Help for it !   Drivel-dom saith —
    (Puffing of impious breath,
    Piping of idiot-breath,) —
Hark to the stormy answer !
    The Cyclone's terrible breath
    Booming judgment and death —
Do ye know it now ? — 'tis the Sansar,
    Dark, icy Wind of Death !

Aid or grace for it? — nay!
(Hear the wild wings in the van —
   Azrael swoops yon way,
Bearing the Infinite Ban!)
   The boughs, how they groan and sway,
   The leaves, how they strip and fray!
Hideous to God and man,
   Know, its doom is to-day —
Shore it up, if ye can!
   Stand from it, while ye may!

Prop and guy? — craze and folly!
   Allah, All-Tender, launches
Levin, volley on volley,
   Full on the curséd branches —
   Blighting the wretched fruit,
Blasting the seed forever —
Earth, with axe and with lever,
   Storms in siege at the root.

Grand and terrible clamor!
Clang of helve and of hammer!
Ah, the thunder of sledges,
   The groaning of winches,
     Cracking of wedges!
It totters, the Wicked Tree,
Like some tall pirate at sea
   Foundering by inches, —
(Gone rail and rudder!)
Ha! dost thou shudder

In thine arcanum?
Tremble, Jehanum!

Was't all a dream of the Past,
    Diluvium's Tidal Wave
  Lifting dreadful and vast?
      Gomorrah's sulphury shroud?
        Egypt's billowy grave?
          Doom of Korah and Dathan?
    Sire of Treason misproud!
What, once more, at the last,
All amort and aghast?
      Have at thee, Sathan!

'Tis but a cycle whirled,
Since, out of the Under-World,
    Swarmed the fiend-whispers, boasting,
Go to, while yon is standing,
Still shall we snuff our branding,
    Our flaying, and our roasting!
  (So crooned the Infernal Seven);
And he waxed so haught and high,
The wretched were fain to cry,
With Spartacus, left to die,
    There is not a God in the heaven!
  (Thus, too, still mooted the Seven,
    Ever they hug that blunder) —
  Lo! the glare of the Levin!
    Hark to the roll of the Thunder!

A groan from the depths ! — ('tis Tophet's —
  The Jezebel-Fury Faints !)
Ah, thou that stonest the prophets,
  And drinkest the blood of saints !
To-night art thou sore afraid
  For thine earth-grown Eidolon ? — (Lo,
  How the Winds of Judgment blow !)
  Aye, the mass begins to go,
At the very scar the blade
Of the stern old Woodman made,
  Scant a score of moons ago.

  Roar wilder, blast !
  Blows, thunder fast !
Each cruel fibre relaxes —
  The cable-roots crack,
  The Trunk's huge wrack
Rings to a million axes.

  Measure your strokes right well —
(Warely, 'tis nigh in sunder !)
  A single blow shall tell —
He topples ! — aye, stand from under !
Crashing, thunder on thunder,
  The Hulk goes down to its hell !
Ah, the horror and wonder,
  The sickness at heart of hell !

But over its sunken ashes,
In opal and emerald flashes,

(Babes of death and of dust,)
Amaranth, Immortelle,
  Lift their sweet lids in trust,
  Smile to the Infinite Trust —
Moly and Asphodel
Bloom o'er the buried hell,
  And joy the Arisen Just.

March, 1862.

ONE WORD.

SPEAK to us, to-day, O Father!
  Our hearts are strangely stirred —
A Nation's Life is hanging
  On a yet unspoken word.

Long, by the hearthstone corner,
  May the aged grandame sit,
And toil, with trembling fingers,
  That another sock be knit;

Men may march and manœuvre,
  And camp on fields of death —
The Iron Saurians wheel and dart,
  And thunder their fiery breath;

But one brave word is wanting —
  The word whose tone should start
The pulses of men to flamelets
  Thrilling through every heart !

O Father, trust your children !
  If ever you found them fail,
'Twas but for lack of the one true word
  That must to the end prevail.

Where funeral willows quiver
On the banks of the Mighty River,
  'Twas seen what men may do —
Flame ahead, and flame to larboard !
  (Aye, the Pit's mouth burned blue !)
Not a craven thought was harbored —
'Twas hell to port and starboard,
  But the Hearts of Oak went through !

They have shown what men may do,
  They have proved how men may die —
Count, who can, the fields they've pressed,
  Each face to the solemn sky !

Is it yet forgotten, of Shiloh
  And the long outnumbered lines,
How the blue frocks lay in winrows ?
  How they died at the Seven Pines ?

How they sank in the Varuna?
  (Seven Foes in Flame around !)
How they went down with the Cumberland,
  Firing, cheering as they drowned ?

Spirits, a hundred of thousands,
  Eager, and bold, and true,
Gone to make good one brave, just word —
  Father, they died for you !

Died, in tempest of battle,
  Died, in the cot's dull pain —
Let their ghosts be glad in heaven,
  That they died — and not in vain !

And never fear but the living
  Shall stand, to the last, by thee —
They shall yet make up the million,
  And another, if need there be !

But fail not, as thy trust is heaven,
  To breathe the word shall wake
The holiest fire of a Nation's heart —
  Speak it, for Christ's dear sake !

Speak it, our earthly Father !
  In the Name of His, and smile
At one breath more of the Viper
  Whose fangs shall crash on the file !

The Angel-Songs are forever,
   The Snake can hiss but his day —
Speak, O Shepherd of Peoples !
   And fold earth's blessings for aye.

July 27th, 1862.

ONLY A WORD.

AYE, one word ! — and forever ends
   The Judas-counsel of fair false friends,
Ends the doubt and the vain debate,
Ends the weary tangle of state.
Ends forever the troublous ghost
Of fleet or file from the Old World coast,
(Borne o'er the shuddering seas to swell
The waning squadrons of Death and Hell) —
And a Nation springs once more to the fight,
With the deathless war-cry of "God and Right !"

SOMNIA CŒLI.

(JANUARY 1, 1863.)

DOOM of Hate and of Darkness!
    Dawn of Life and of Light!
Surely, 'twas God's fair Angel
    Stood by my couch, last night.

Looked on the careworn Creature,
    Pitied the yearning Dust —
I slept the sleep of the Blesséd,
    Dreamed the dreams of the Just.

O, griefs of our Infant Being,
    O, earthly anguish and ills,
All at an end, and forever! —
    I stood on the Happy Hills.

The hills and the fields of Beulah
    Fair in the Heavenly Sun!
Calm, and peace, and forgiveness —
    Life and Death were at one.

Vale and forest grew dimmer,
   Cliff gloomed purple and gray —
And slowly a night descended
   More sweet than our sunniest day.

But far in the lost horizon,
   Through the Outer Darkness whirled
A vast and a wretched Shadow —
   Methought, 'twas this our world.

Ah, the gloom and the horror!
   For the Powers of Air had met —
And the spears of Dawn and of Death-Eclipse
   In deadly battle were set.

Smoke, and shudder, and torment!
   Crash, and rending, and wrack! —
And if ever the Light seemed gaining,
   The Dark still trampled it back.

Had I passed the Shining Portal,
   Which the Lovelier Land doth keep?
Ah, nay! — for these eyes were mortal,
   And they could not choose but weep.

But, lifting the lids of anguish,
   I was 'ware, by the waning light,
Of a grand and a holy Presence,
   Calm and strong, in my sight.

Grace, and gladness, and splendor !
   Pity, 'mid power and pride ! —
(Yet, methought, more truly tender
   A dimmer Form at his side,
Lovely, pallid, and slender,
   Sweetly and sadly eyed.)

And the glorious Lips bespake me,
   With a smile, as half in mirth,
Questioning — what the trouble
   Wearies thee, Child of Earth !

What thereto could I answer?
   What but, with sigh and tear —
All, alas, is so wretched there !
   All is so happy here !

But again the word was taken —
   Therefore art thou forlorn ?
How dreamest thou what the angels,
   In their earthly day, have borne ?

How weary their earlier way,
   While yon half-made orb they trod —
The blinder reason, the dimmer ray,
   The ruder working of God.

For 'tis raised, the tempest of trouble,
   (Though seeming judgment or curse,)
Of the infinite Love and Pity —
   And ever to thwart a worse.

The whirl, the crash, and the ruin,
  (Much though it seem to thee,)
Is naught but a broken toy of earth
  To the horror that else should be !

Were it better, the Lord's fair Garden
  Of its fruitage forever fail —
That a growth of drowsy venom
  Still fester for slug and snail —
Or that Crime, the monstrous Mandrake,
  Be rooted with shriek and wail ?

That Hell, unchallenged forever,
  Craze yon Sphere-Soul past doubt —
Or Earth, possessed of her Demon,
  Be rent in the casting out ?

Hereon 'twere idle to linger.
  True, that offence must come —
Woe, ah woe to the bringer !
  (But the gentler Shade was dumb.)

He spake — but shadow and thunder
  Swept o'er the unhappy sphere —
And a low, dull throb thereunder
  Trembled on heart and ear —

A hollow, heavy pulsation,
  As from filling of trench and grave —
And a deeper ululation

Up through the dark did wave —
The moan of a Mother-Nation
  For her darling and her brave.

Ever from earth ascended
  The thrill and shudder of pain —
When shall thy grief be ended,
  O Earth? — and I wept again.

Is it ever of woe and anguish
  That the better world is born?
Ever a night of dreadful dream
  Must cradle the Holy Morn?

Thus I mourned and lamented,
  With the wearied heart of a child,
'Feared, lest never the day should dawn —
  But again the Presence smiled,

And again, as in cheer, he spake —
  Aye, ever yon Cradle-Sphere
Is rudely rocked ere the Earth-Soul wake —
  But another rule is here,
And a Morn of joy no shadow may break
  But 'tokens a happier Year.

And therewith pleaded the Other —
  Is it so unhappy then,
To die for God and for Mother,
  Rendering the soul like men?

Is it grievous, weapon in hand
   For Faith and the Holy Name,
To pass, in strength, to the wondrous Land,
   By the Portal of Steel and Flame?

Thunder, to-day, at the Outer Gate!
   Earth's eager squadrons form —
The daring spirits that could not wait
   Are taking Heaven by storm!

The splendor of battle in their eyes,
   They enter, even now —
How it lights the Port of Paradise,
   The death-gleam on each brow!

The fire on the wan cheek flickered,
   The form was in act to fleet —
Yet again the Voice made murmur,
   (It was strangely low and sweet,)
Not thine, as yet, even here, to mark
   How Life and Death may meet.

Nor mine, to-night, to whisper
   The word could set thee free —
They faded, the mighty Brothers,
   As Twin-Clouds fade o'er the sea —
Yet murmured still, in their going,
   Peace, O mortal, with thee!
Sleep, and dream the salvation
   Thine eyes, the morn, shall see.
     5*

And therewith peace waved o'er me —
  The mighty morning broke,
From fevered slumber and guilty dream
  The Land, in wonder, woke —
It rocked and rang to the noblest Word
  Ever a mortal spoke !

Though these our changes and choices
  But falter the Will Divine, —
Of all the infinite voices
  That throng to the Central Shrine,
None, O father, rejoices
  Heaven, to the heart, like thine !

A touch from the Unseen Finger,
  Lo, they kindle, the lips of clay —
Ah, for a worthier singer ! —
  Joy thee, O earth ! — to-day,
(Though awhile it seem to linger,)
  The Shadow passes — for aye !

Thy murky Shroud to the Gone shall sweep
  On the wings of the Thunder-Gale —
The Share of the Lord is driving deep,
  But blossom nor fruit shall fail.

And now, come wrath and reviling !
  Let the Crime rave as it can,
With the yelp of pettier treason,

The caitiff cursing and ban —
We know that a God is in Heaven,
  We know that Earth has a Man!

Let them gloat, the ravined Nations,
  Scenting our blood through the dark,
(As his fellows glare 'mid the salt-sea,
  Ere they tear at a wounded shark.)

Let it gnash, the rage and the menace,
  And the gnarring, o'er and o'er,
Like a mangled Wolf's, from out yon gloom —
  Telling, as time afore,
Murder doth not go to the doom
  Without a Death-Shrill the more !

Come, battle of stormiest breath,
  O'er meadow and hill-side brown
The long lines sweeping up to death,
  'Mid thunder from trench and town —
The victor cheer, or the martyr faith
  For Right and for God's Renown !

And come, the shock and the shudder !
  The dull and heavy heart-pain,
The watch, the woe, and the waiting —
  Once more, like the summer's rain,
Pour thy dear blood, beloved Land ! —
  Never a drop is in vain !

And never in vain, our brothers !
   That dark December's day,
For the Truth, and for hope to others,
   By slope and by trench ye lay —

Lay, through the long night's damp,
   On a lost and fatal field ;
But a stronger Line, and a vaster Camp
   To your noble charge did yield.

Did we deem 'twas woe and pity
   That there, in your flower, ye died ?
Ah, fond I — the Celestial City
   Her Portal fair flung wide.

The mighty Avenue surges —
   For, to-day, doth enter in
An Army of victor souls and strong,
   Sublimed, through fire, from sin.

And their ranks form deep for escort,
   The holy and valiant Throng
Erst risen, through storm and battle,
   Guarding the Good 'gainst Wrong.

The Colors ye bore in vain that day
   Yet wave o'er Heaven's Recruits —
And are trooped by Aidenn's starriest Gate,
   While the Flaming Sword salutes !

January, 1863.

THE BATTLE OF CHARLESTOWN.

(December 2, 1859.)

FRESH palms for the Old Dominion!
　　New peers for the valiant Dead!
Never hath showered her sunshine
　　On a field of doughtier dread —
Heroes in buff three thousand,
　　And a single scarred gray head!

Fuss, and feathers, and flurry —
　　Clink, and rattle, and roar —
The old man looks around him
　　On meadow and mountain hoar;
The place, he remarks, is pleasant,
　　I had not seen it before.

Form, in your boldest order,
　　Let the people press no nigher!
Would ye have them hear to his words —
　　The words that may spread like fire?

'Tis a right smart chance to test him —
　　(Here we are at the gallows-tree,)
So knot the noose — pretty tightly —
　　Bandage his eyes — and we'll see,

(For we'll keep him waiting a little,)
    If he tremble in nerve or knee.

There, in a string, we've got him!
    (Shall the music bang and blow?)
The chivalry wheels and marches,
    And airs its valor below.

Look hard in the blindfold visage,
    (He can't look back,) and inquire,
(He has stood there nearly a quarter,)
    If he doesn't begin to tire?

Not yet! how long will he keep us,
    To see if he quail or no?
I reckon it's no use waiting,
    And 'tis time that we had the show.

For the trouble — we can't see why —
    Seems with us, and not with him,
As he stands 'neath the autumn sky,
    So strangely solemn and dim!

But high let our standard flout it!
    "Sic semper" — the drop comes down —
And, (woe to the rogues that doubt it!)
    There's an end of old John Brown!

December 5th, 1859.

HONEST ABE.

(NOMINATION OF 1860.)

"*A most hideous nickname.*"

"HONEST ABE!" What strange vexation
　　Thrills an office-armchaired party!
What impatience and disgust
That the people should put trust
　　In a name so true and hearty!
What indignant lamentation
　　For the unchosen — surely fitter
　　(Growl they) than a rough rail-splitter —
Most unheard-of nomination!

If the name you chance to mention,
Sir (they splutter) the Convention,
　　Sir, has acted like a babe!
You have missed it, be assured,
All your best men left to leeward;
Give us Banks, or Bates, or Seward, —
　　But confound this "HONEST ABE!"

There's a story somewhere told,
By a fellow grave and old,
　　Which, just now, is rather pat.

I bethink me of his name —
Plutarch — and of lives the same
   Had as many as a cat.

In the little State of Athens
   Was a usage, there and then
Practised by those classic heathens,
   Rather hard on public men.
Whatsoe'er the service past,
   If they happened to distrust 'em —
Thought 'em getting on too fast —
   'Twas, it seems, the pleasant custom
Just an oyster-shell to shy
(*Sans* a wherefore or a why)
Into a ballot-box huge and high —
   With whatever name upon it
Chanced the elector's mind to strike,
   (Sulking, like a jealous noddy,
   O'er his Norwalks and his toddy,) —
   Well — the name of anybody
That he didn't chance to like.
   And the gentleman who won it —
Such election — (held to tell
   What the free enlightened wished) —
   Was, in fact, considered dished,
And served out on the half-shell !
   And must needs, at any rate,
Draw a line in double-quick,
Mizzle, *vamos*, cut his stick,
   And absquatulate !

Simple and ingenious scheme !
  Of split tickets there were none —
(Though the bivalve you might deem
Suited well for such extreme) —
  Hard or Soft Shell — all was one !

Once, while thus with general clamor
  Athens eased her factious heart —
When the smith forsook his hammer,
  And the huckster left his mart —

Past the scene of noisy riot,
  Clatter of shells and windy talk,
Aristides, calm and quiet,
  Chanced to take a morning walk.

Musing, in his wonted fashion,
  On the double care of state —
On the Demos' fickle passion,
  And the cold patrician hate ;

When a voter pressed beside him,
  Saying, " Stranger, can you spell
Aristides ? Wal, jest write him,
  Square and straight, on this here shell."

Smiling, cheery as a cricket,
  Wrote the old Republican —
Then, as he returned the ticket,
  Asked — " And what's his crime, my man ? "

"Wal, not much," said Snooks, appearing
    Puzzled, " only I'll be cussed
But I'm sick to death of hearing
    That old critter called 'THE JUST'!"

THE CAMP OF NOVEMBER.

(ELECTION OF 1856.)

FAST o'er the desert rode Fremont,
    O'er the broad and burning plain —
By the Bitter Lake, and the frozen font
    In the wild Nevada's chain.
The wolf howled long round his lonely camp,
The mist of morning was cold and damp,
And the dark Platte foamed o'er his charger's neck
Ere he stood on the grand Sierra's Peak.

    There's a blacker tide to stem, my boys !
        There's a rougher hill to climb !
    We shall camp 'mid faction's snarling noise,
        And the howl of startled crime.
There's work to do ere we gain the goal —
There are logs and lumps from our track to roll —
There are mules to spur — there are wolves to scare
From the prey they gorge in their bloody lair.

Do we wait to drink of a bitterer cup?
    Or clamor for darker proof?
The corse lies stark, and the smoke goes up
    From the settler's burning roof—
Our brothers faint on the far-off plains,
Their blood lies fresh 'neath the Autumn rains.
Are we yet to pause? do we linger till
The slave-roll is called on Bunker Hill?

    Too long have we stood in idle doubt—
    Too blind and deaf we have been
    To the foul assault that foamed without,
    And the fouler treason within.
But the clock is striking the final hour
Of fools in office and knaves in power.
From their place of crime they shall slink away,
Like guilty ghosts at the dawn of day.

    The Dagon that lords it o'er our land,
    Have at him, one and all!
    Let us league like brothers, heart and hand,
    Till the monstrous idol fall.
Tumble him down to rot away,
With his front of brass and his feet of clay.
Stand, and our children yet shall see
Not an inch of soil but is fair and free.

    Let us prove the right that men may do,
    Let us march to the Union's tread—
    We are led by one that is tried and true,
    And we're watched by One o'erhead.

The camp-fire shining to cheer our toil
Shall never be kindled on servile soil.
The land that was bought with our father's graves
Shall never be trod or tilled by slaves!

ABRAHAM LINCOLN.

(SUMMER, 1865.)

DEAD is the roll of the drums,
  And the distant thunders die,
 They fade in the far-off sky;
And a lovely summer comes,
  Like the smile of Him on high.

Lulled, the storm and the onset.
  Earth lies in a sunny swoon;
  Stiller splendor of noon,
Softer glory of sunset,
  Milder starlight and moon!

For the kindly Seasons love us;
  They smile over trench and clod,
(Where we left the bravest of us,) —
  There's a brighter green of the sod,
And a holier calm above us
  In the blesséd Blue of God.

The roar and ravage were vain ;
  And Nature, that never yields,
Is busy with sun and rain
At her old sweet work again   .
  On the lonely battle-fields.

How the tall white daisies grow,
  Where the grim artillery rolled !
(Was it only a moon ago ?
  It seems a century old,) —

And the bee hums in the clover,
  As the pleasant June comes on ;
Aye, the wars are all over, —
  But our good Father is gone.

There was tumbling of traitor fort,
  Flaming of traitor fleet —
Lighting of city and port,
  Clasping in square and street.

There was thunder of mine and gun,
  Cheering by mast and tent, —
When — his dread work all done,
And his high fame full won —
  Died the Good President.

In his quiet chair he sate,
  Pure of malice or guile,
Stainless of fear or hate, —
  And there played a pleasant smile

On the rough and careworn face ;
  For his heart was all the while
On means of mercy and grace.

The brave old Flag drooped o'er him,
  (A fold in the hard hand lay,) —
  He looked, perchance, on the play, —
But the scene was a shadow before him,
  For his thoughts were far away.

'Twas but the morn, (yon fearful
  Death-shade, gloomy and vast,
  Lifting slowly at last,)
  His household heard him say,
" 'Tis long since I've been so cheerful,
  So light of heart as to-day."

'Twas dying, the long dread clang, —
  But, or ever the blesséd ray
  Of peace could brighten to day,
  Murder stood by the way —
Treason struck home his fang !
One throb — and, without a pang,
  That pure soul passed away.

Idle, in this our blindness,
  To marvel we cannot see
  Wherefore such things should be ;
Or to question Infinite Kindness
  Of this or of that Decree.

Or to fear lest Nature bungle,
   That in certain ways she errs, —
The cobra in the jungle,
    The crotalus in the sod,
  Evil and good are hers, —
  Murderers and torturers !
    Ye, too, were made by God.

All slowly heaven is nighing,
  Needs that offence must come ;
Ever the Old Wrong dying
Will sting, in the death-coil lying,
   And hiss till its fork be dumb.

But dare deny no further,
  Black-hearted, brazen-cheeked !
Ye on whose lips yon murther
  These fifty moons hath reeked, —

From the wretched scenic dunce,
  Long a-hungered to rouse
A Nation's heart for the nonce, —
(Hugging his hell, so that once
  He might yet bring down the house !) —

From the commons, gross and simple,
  Of a blind and bloody land,
    (Long fed on venomous lies !) —
  To the horrid heart and hand
   That sumless murder dyes —

The hand that drew the wimple
   Over those cruel eyes.

Pass on, — your deeds are done,
Forever sets your sun ;
   Vainly ye lived or died,
'Gainst Freedom and the Laws, —
And your memory and your cause
   Shall haunt o'er the trophied tide

Like some Pirate Caravel floating
   Dreadful, adrift — whose crew
From her yard-arms dangle rotting —
   The old Horror of the blue.

Avoid ye, — let the morrow
   Sentence or mercy see.
Pass to your place : our sorrow
Is all too dark to borrow
   One shade from such as ye.

But if one, with merciful eyes,
From the forgiving skies
   Looks, 'mid our gloom, to see
Yonder where Murder lies,
Stripped of the woman guise,
   And waiting the doom — 'tis he.

Kindly Spirit ! — Ah, when did treason
   Bid such a generous nature cease,

Mild by temper and strong by reason,
   But ever leaning to love and peace?

A head how sober; a heart how spacious;
   A manner equal with high or low;
Rough but gentle, uncouth but gracious,
   And still inclining to lips of woe.

Patient when saddest, calm when sternest,
   Grieved when rigid for justice' sake;
Given to jest, yet ever in earnest
   If aught of right or truth were at stake.

Simple of heart, yet shrewd therewith,
   Slow to resolve, but firm to hold;
Still with parable and with myth
   Seasoning truth, like Them of old;
Aptest humor and quaintest pith!
   (Still we smile o'er the tales he told.)

And if, sometimes, in saddest stress,
   That mind, over-meshed by fate,
   (Ringed round with treason and hate,
And guiding the State by guess,)
   Could doubt and could hesitate —
Who, alas, had done less
   In the world's most deadly strait?

But how true to the Common Cause!
   Of his task how unweary!

6

How hard he worked, how good he was,
  How kindly and cheery !

How, while it marked redouble
  The howls and hisses and sneers,
That great heart bore our trouble
  Through all these terrible years ;

And, cooling passion with state,
  And ever counting the cost,
Kept the Twin World-Robbers in wait
  Till the time for their clutch was lost.

How much he cared for the State,
  How little for praise or pelf !
A man too simply great
  To scheme for his proper self.

But in mirth that strong heart rested
  From its strife with the false and violent, —
A jester ! — So Henry jested,
  So jested William the Silent.

Orange, shocking the dull
  With careless conceit and quip,
Yet holding the dumb heart full
  With Holland's life on his lip ! [13]

Navarre, bonhomme and pleasant,
  Pitying the poor man's lot,

Wishing that every peasant
  A chicken had in his pot ;

Feeding the stubborn bourgeois,
  Though Paris still held out ;
Holding the League in awe,
  But jolly with all about.

Out of an o'erflowed fulness
  Those deep hearts seemed too light, —
(And so 'twas, murder's dulness
  Was set with sullener spite.)

Yet whoso might pierce the guise
  Of mirth in the man we mourn,
Would mark, and with grieved surprise,
  All the great soul had borne,
In the piteous lines, and the kind, sad eyes
  So dreadfully wearied and worn.

And we trusted, (the last dread page
  Once turned, of our Dooms-day Scroll,)
  To have seen him, sunny of soul,
In a cheery, grand old age.

But, Father, 'tis well with thee !
  And since ever, when God draws nigh,
Some grief for the good must be,
  'Twas well, even so to die, —

'Mid the thunder of Treason's fall,
  The yielding of haughty town,
The crashing of cruel wall,
  The trembling of tyrant crown !

The ringing of hearth and pavement
  To the clash of falling chains, —
The centuries of enslavement
  Dead, with their blood-bought gains !

And through trouble weary and long
  Well hadst thou seen the way,
Leaving the State so strong
  It did not reel for a day ;

And even in death couldst give
  A token for Freedom's strife —
A proof how republics live,
  And not by a single life,

But the Right Divine of man,
  And the many, trained to be free, —
And none, since the world began,
  Ever was mourned like thee.

Dost thou feel it, O noble Heart !
  (So grieved and so wronged below,)
From the rest wherein thou art ?
Do they see it, those patient eyes ?
Is there heed in the happy skies
  For tokens of world-wide woe ?

The Land's great lamentations,
  The mighty mourning of cannon,
    The myriad flags half-mast —
The late remorse of the nations,
  Grief from Volga to Shannon !
    (Now they know thee at last.)

How, from gray Niagara's shore
  To Canaveral's surfy shoal —
From the rough Atlantic roar
  To the long Pacific roll —
  For bereavement and for dole,
Every cottage wears its weed,
  White as thine own pure soul,
And black as the traitor deed.

How, under a nation's pall,
  The dust so dear in our sight
    To its home on the prairie past, —
The leagues of funeral,
  The myriads, morn and night,
    Pressing to look their last.

Nor alone the State's Eclipse ;
  But how tears in hard eyes gather —
And on rough and bearded lips,
Of the regiments and the ships —
  "Oh, our dear Father !"

And methinks of all the million
  That looked on the dark dead face,

'Neath its sable-plumed pavilion,
　　The crone of a humbler race
Is saddest of all to think on,
　　And the old swart lips that said,
Sobbing, " Abraham Lincoln !
　　Oh, he is dead, he is dead ! "

Hush ! let our heavy souls
　　To-day be glad ; for agen
The stormy music swells and rolls,
　　Stirring the hearts of men.

And under the Nation's Dome,
　　They've guarded so well and long,
Our boys come marching home,
　　Two hundred thousand strong.

All in the pleasant month of May,
　　With war-worn colors and drums,
Still, through the livelong summer's day,
　　Regiment, regiment comes.

Like the tide, yesty and barmy,
　　That sets on a wild lee-shore,
Surge the ranks of an army
　　Never reviewed before !

Who shall look on the like agen,
　　Or see such host of the brave ?
A mighty River of marching men

Rolls the Capital through —
Rank on rank, and wave on wave,
   Of bayonet-crested blue !

How the chargers neigh and champ,
(Their riders weary of camp,)
   With curvet and with caracole ! —
The cavalry comes with thundrous tramp,
   And the cannons heavily roll.

And ever, flowery and gay,
The Staff sweeps on in a spray
   Of tossing forelocks and manes ;
But each bridle-arm has a weed
Of funeral, black as the steed
   That fiery Sheridan reins.

Grandest of mortal sights
   The sun-browned ranks to view —
The Colors ragg'd in a hundred fights,
   And the dusty Frocks of Blue !

And all day, mile on mile,
With cheer, and waving, and smile,
The war-worn legions defile
   Where the nation's noblest stand ;
And the Great Lieutenant looks on,
   With the Flower of a rescued Land, —
For the terrible work is done,
And the Good Fight is won
   For God and for Fatherland.

So, from the fields they win,
　　Our men are marching home,
　　A million are marching home !
To the cannon's thundering din,
　　And banners on mast and dome, —
And the ships come sailing in
　　With all their ensigns dight,
　　As erst for a great sea-fight.

Let every color fly,
　　Every pennon flaunt in pride ;
Wave, Starry Flag, on high !
Float in the sunny sky,
　　Stream o'er the stormy tide !
For every stripe of stainless hue,
And every star in the field of blue,
Ten thousand of the brave and true
　　Have laid them down and died.

And in all our pride to-day
　　We think, with a tender pain,
Of those so far away
　　They will not come home again.

And our boys had fondly thought,
　　To-day, in marching by,
From the ground so dearly bought,
And the fields so bravely fought,
　　To have met their Father's eye.

But they may not see him in place,
   Nor their ranks be seen of him ;
We look for the well-known face,
   And the splendor is strangely dim.

Perished ? — who was it said
   Our Leader had passed away ?
Dead ? Our President dead ?
   He has not died for a day !

We mourn for a little breath
   Such as, late or soon, dust yields ;
But the Dark Flower of Death
   Blooms in the fadeless fields.

We looked on a cold, still brow,
   But Lincoln could yet survive ;
   He never was more alive,
Never nearer than now.

For the pleasant season found him,
   Guarded by faithful hands,
   In the fairest of Summer Lands ;
With his own brave Staff around him,
   There our President stands.

There they are all at his side,
   The noble hearts and true,
   That did all men might do —
Then slept, with their swords, and died.

Of little the storm has reft us
  But the brave and kindly clay —
('Tis but dust where Lander left us,
  And but turf where Lyon lay.)

There's Winthrop, true to the end,
  And Ellsworth of long ago,
  (First fair young head laid low !)
There's Baker, the brave old friend,
  And Douglas, the friendly foe.

(Baker, that still stood up
  When 'twas death on either hand ;
" 'Tis a soldier's part to stoop,
  But the Senator must stand.")

The heroes gather and form, —
  There's Cameron, with his scars,
Sedgwick, of siege and storm,
  And Mitchell, that joined his stars.

Winthrop, of sword and pen,
  Wadsworth, with silver hair,
Mansfield, ruler of men,
  And brave McPherson are there.

Birney, who led so long,
  Abbott, born to command,
Elliott the bold, and Strong,
  Who fell on the hard-fought strand.

Lytle, soldier and bard,
  And the Ellets, sire and son —
Ransom, all grandly scarred,
And Redfield, no more on guard,
  (But Alatoona is won !)

Reno, of pure desert,
  Kearney, with heart of flame,
And Russell, that hid his hurt
  Till the final death-bolt came ;

Terrill, dead where he fought,
  Wallace, that would not yield,
And Sumner, who vainly sought
  A grave on the foughten field,

(But died ere the end he saw,
  With years and battles outworn:)
There's Harmon of Kenesaw,
And Ulric Dahlgren, and Shaw,
  That slept with his Hope Forlorn.

Bayard, that knew not fear,
  (True as the knight of yore,)
And Putnam, and Paul Revere,
  Worthy the names they bore.

Allen, who died for others,
  Bryan, of gentle fame,
And the brave New England brothers
  That have left us Lowell's name.

Home, at last, from the wars, —
 Stedman, the staunch and mild,
 And Janeway, our hero-child,
Home, with his fifteen scars !

There's Porter, ever in front,
 True son of a sea-king sire,
And Christian Foote, and Dupont,
(Dupont, who led his ships
Rounding the first Ellipse
 Of thunder and of fire.)

There's Ward, with his brave death-wounds,
 And Cummings, of spotless name,
And Smith, who hurtled his rounds
 When deck and hatch were aflame ;

Wainwright, steadfast and true,
 Rodgers, of brave sea-blood,
And Craven, with ship and crew
 Sunk in the salt sea flood.

And, a little later to part,
 Our Captain, noble and dear —
(Did they deem thee, then, austere ?
Drayton ! — O pure and kindly heart !
 Thine is the seaman's tear.)

All such, — and many another,
 (Ah, list how long to name !)

That stood like brother by brother,
　And died on the field of fame.

And around — (for there can cease
　This earthly trouble) — they throng,
The friends that had passed in peace,
　The foes that have seen their wrong.

(But, a little from the rest,
　With sad eyes looking down,
　And brows of softened frown,
With stern arms on the chest,
Are two, standing abreast —
　Stonewall and Old John Brown.)

But the stainless and the true,
　These by their President stand,
To look on his last review,
　Or march with the old command.

And lo, from a thousand fields,
　From all the old battle-haunts,
A greater Army than Sherman wields,
　A grander Review than Grant's !

Gathered home from the grave,
　Risen from sun and rain —
Rescued from wind and wave
　Out of the stormy main —
The Legions of our Brave
　Are all in their lines again !

Many a stout Corps that went,
Full-ranked, from camp and tent,
   And brought back a brigade ;
Many a brave regiment,
   That mustered only a squad.

The lost battalions,
   That, when the fight went wrong,
Stood and died at their guns, —
   The stormers steady and strong,

With their best blood that bought
   Scarp, and ravelin, and wall, —
The companies that fought
   Till a corporal's guard was all.

Many a valiant crew,
   That passed in battle and wreck, —
Ah, so faithful and true !
   They died on the bloody deck,
They sank in the soundless blue.

All the loyal and bold
   That lay on a soldier's bier, —
   The stretchers borne to the rear,
The hammocks lowered to the hold.

The shattered wreck we hurried,
   In death-fight, from deck and port, —
The Blacks that Wagner buried —
   That died in the Bloody Fort !

Comrades of camp and mess,
  Left, as they lay, to die,
In the battle's sorest stress,
  When the storm of fight swept by, —
They lay in the Wilderness,
  Ah, where did they not lie ?

In the tangled swamp they lay,
  They lay so still on the sward ! —
They rolled in the sick-bay,
Moaning their lives away —
  They flushed in the fevered ward.

They rotted in Libby yonder,
  They starved in the foul stockade —
Hearing afar the thunder
  Of the Union cannonade !

But the old wounds all are healed,
  And the dungeoned limbs are free, —
The Blue Frocks rise from the field,
  The Blue Jackets out of the sea.

They've 'scaped from the torture-den,
  They've broken the bloody sod,
They're all come to life agen ! —
The Third of a Million men
  That died for Thee and for God !

A tenderer green than May
  The Eternal Season wears, —

The blue of our summer's day
  Is dim and pallid to theirs, —
The Horror faded away,
  And 'twas heaven all unawares !

Tents on the Infinite Shore !
  Flags in the azuline sky,
Sails on the seas once more !
  To-day, in the heaven on high,
All under arms once more !

The troops are all in their lines,
  The guidons flutter and play ;
But every bayonet shines,
  For all must march to-day.

What lofty pennons flaunt ?
What mighty echoes haunt,
  As of great guns, o'er the main ?
  Hark to the sound again —
The Congress is all a-taunt !
  'The Cumberland's manned again !

All the ships and their men
  Are in line of battle to-day, —
All at quarters, as when
  Their last roll thundered away, —
All at their guns, as then,
  For the Fleet salutes to-day.

The armies have broken camp
  On the vast and sunny plain,
  The drums are rolling again ;
With steady, measured tramp,
  They're marching all again.

With alignment firm and. solemn,
  Once again they form
In mighty square and column, —
  But never for charge and storm.

The Old Flag they died under
  Floats above them on the shore,
And on the great ships yonder
  The ensigns dip once more —
And once again the thunder
  Of the thirty guns and four !

In solid platoons of steel,
  Under heaven's triumphal arch,
The long lines break and wheel —
  And the word is, "Forward, march !"

The Colors ripple o'erhead,
  The drums roll up to the sky,
And with martial time and tread
  The regiments all pass by —
The ranks of our faithful Dead,
  Meeting their President's eye.

With a soldier's quiet pride
   They smile o'er the perished pain,
   For their anguish was not vain —
For thee, O Father, we died !
   And we did not die in vain.

March on, your last brave mile !
   Salute him, Star and Lace,
Form round him, rank and file,
   And look on the kind, rough face ;
But the quaint and homely smile
   Has a glory and a grace
It never had known erewhile —
   Never, in time and space.

Close round him, hearts of pride !
Press near him, side by side, —
   Our Father is not alone !
For the Holy Right ye died,
And Christ, the Crucified,
   Waits to welcome his own

MISCELLANEOUS POEMS.

PSYCHAURA.

THE wind of an autumn midnight
   Is moaning around my door —
The curtains wave at the window,
   The carpet lifts on the floor.

There are sounds like startled footfalls
   In the distant chambers now,
And the touching of airy fingers
   Is busy on hand and brow:

'Tis thus, in the Soul's dark dwelling —
   By the moody host unsought —
Through the chambers of memory wander
   The invisible airs of thought.

For it bloweth where it listeth,
   With a murmur loud or low ;
Whence it cometh — whither it goeth —
   None tell us, and none may know.

Now wearying round the portals
   Of the vacant, desolate mind —
As the doors of a ruined mansion,
   That creak in the cold night wind.

And anon an awful memory
   Sweeps over it fierce and high —
Like the roar of a mountain forest
   When the midnight gale goes by.

Then its voice subsides in wailing,
   And, ere the dawning of day,
Murmuring fainter and fainter,
   In the distance dies away.

OLD PAPERS.

AS who, in idly searching o'er
      Some seldom-entered garret shed,
Might, with strange pity, touch the poor
   Moth-eaten garments of the dead, —

Thus, (to their wearer once allied,) .
   I lift these weeds of buried woe —
These relics of a Self that died
   So sadly and so long ago.

'Tis said that seven short years can change,
　　Through nerve and bone, this knitted frame, —
Cellule by cellule waxing strange,
　　Till not an atom is the same.

By what more subtle, slow degrees,
　　Thus may the mind transmute its all,
That calmly it should dwell on these,
　　As on another's fate and fall !

So far remote from joy or bale,
　　Wherewith each dusky page is rife,
I seem to read some piteous tale
　　Of romance, true unto the life.

Too daring thoughts ! too idle deeds !
　　A soul that questioned, loved, and sinned !
And hopes, that stand like last year's weeds
　　And shudder in the dead March wind !

Grave of gone dreams ! could such convulse
　. Youth's fevered trance ? — The plot grows thick ;
Was it this cold and even pulse
　　That thrilled with life so fierce and quick ?

Well, I can smile at all this now, —
　　But cannot smile when I recall
The heart of faith, the open brow,
　　The trust that once was all in all ; —

Nor when — Ah, faded, spectral sheet !
  Wraith of long-perished wrong and time —
Forbear ! the spirit starts to meet
  The resurrection of its crime !

Starts — from its human world shut out —
  As some detected changeling elf,
Doomed, with strange agony and doubt,
  To enter on his former self.

Ill-omened leaves, still rust apart !
  No further ! — 'tis a page turned o'er,
And the long dead and coffined heart
  Throbs into wretched life once more.

ALL TOGETHER.

OLD friends and dear ! it were ungentle rhyme,
  If I should question of your true hearts,
        whether
Ye have forgotten that far, pleasant time,
  The good old time when we were all together.

Our limbs were lusty and our souls sublime ;
  We never heeded cold and winter weather,
Nor sun nor travel, in that cheery time,
  The brave old time when we were all together.

Pleasant it was to tread the mountain thyme,
 Sweet was the pure and piny mountain ether,
And pleasant all; but this was in the time,
 The good old time when we were all together.

Since then I've strayed through many a fitful clime,
 (Tossed on the wind of fortune like a feather,)
And chanced with rare good fellows in my time —
 But ne'er the time that we have known together :

But none like those brave hearts, (for now I climb
 Gray hills alone, or thread the lonely heather,)
That walked beside me in the ancient time,
 The good old time when we were all together.

Long since, we parted in our careless prime,
 Like summer birds no June shall hasten hither ;
No more to meet as in that merry time,
 The sweet spring-time that shone on all together.

Some, to the fevered city's toil and grime,
 And some o'er distant seas, and some — ah !
  whither ?
Nay, we shall never meet as in the time,
 The dear old time when we were all together.

And some — above their heads, in wind and rime,
 Year after year, the grasses wave and wither ;
Aye, we shall meet ! — 'tis but a little time,
 And all shall lie with folded hands together.

And if, beyond the sphere of doubt and crime,
    Lie purer lands — ah ! let our steps be thither ;
That, done with earthly change and earthly time,
    In God's good time we may be all together.

SUSPIRIA NOCTIS.

READING, and reading — little is the gain
    Long dwelling with the minds of dead men
        leaves.
List rather to the melancholy rain,
                Drop — dropping from the eaves.

Still the old tale — how hardly worth the telling !
    Hark to the wind !— again that mournful sound,
That, all night long, around this lonely dwelling,
                Moans like a dying hound.

TO THE POET.

AYE, doubt, and hope, and dream !
    (Thou canst not choose) — and question the
        Divine !
Thus — since of earth — did They, whose holier
        gleam
    Was clouded erst, as thine.

    Souls that, like Setting Suns,
Have left their radiance flung on sea and shore —
The Wise, the Pure, the Everlasting Ones,
    They who have gone before.

    But muse no more in rhyme !
Lest, haply, fond imaginings and hopes,
In their inception truthful or sublime,
    Perish in wordy tropes.

    In quiet mark them roll,
The grand, still shadows of eternity —
And mighty Thoughts, that move along the soul
    Like clouds upon the sea.

GONE.

GONE — and forever! the grace and glory,
　　The passionate earth-life sweet and strong —
Good and glee are an old-time story,
　　Hope and loving have left for long.

How has it failed, the heart's free fountain !
　　Hand and foot ? — alas, was't these
Leaped the chasm, and climbed the mountain,
　　And held the tiller through stormy seas ?

How has it dwarfed, the soul's high stature !
　　That clasped its darlings of earth and blue —
Knew the divine, or in art or nature,
　　Loved the lovely, and owned the true.

Spirit fordone ! to thy darkening chamber
　　Turn, with the penanced eyes of eld,
Never again to behold the sunshine —
　　Never again till the pulse be quelled.

As when, forlornly, at saddest midnight,
　　The pale, wan lips we shall press no more,
Seen by the cold and colorless moonlight,
　　Tremble farewell — and the dream is o'er ;

Thus, O Life that aspired and longed so!
  All amort, thou hast kissed good-bye,
Good-bye to the Youth was loved and wronged so —
  And a chill, drear morn comes up the sky.

PRESENTIMENT.

STRANGE heaviness — I know not why.
  The old grief, methought, had grown more
      light —
And no new ill hath chanced — yet I
  Am very sorrowful to-night.

It is not that I cannot bear
  The burden countless hearts have borne —
It is not that I shrink to wear
  The garment countless limbs have worn —

Nor that, through sordid care and strife,
  The soul her comrade must sustain,
To draw with pain the breath of life,
  And break their daily bread with pain —

(So fiercely hath it drunk of joy,
  So deeply drained the dregs of woe,
That common grief may scarce annoy,
  And common good were pale and low) —

But that, to-night, from out the throng
   Some surlier shadow flickers still —
Some wraith of old ancestral wrong,
   Or cold rapport of coming ill.

Haunt, an thou will, gray evil gone !
   Thrill, an 'tis thou, dumb pang to be !
The heart can hold ye both at one,
   That knows a sadder guest than ye.

MIDNIGHT—A LAMENT.

DO the dead carry their cares,
   Like us, to the place of rest ?
The long, long night — is it theirs,
   Weary to brain and breast ?
Ah, that I knew how it fares
   With One that I loved the best !

I lie alone in the house.
   How the wretched North-wind raves !
I listen, and think of those
   O'er whose heads the wet grass waves —
Do they hear the wind that blows,
   And the rain on their lonely graves ?

Heads that I helped to lay
  On the pillow that lasts for aye.
It is but a little way
  To the dreary hill where they lie —
No bed but the cold, cold clay —
  No roof but the stormy sky.

Cruel the thought and vain !
  They've now nothing more to bear —
Done with sickness and pain,
  Done with trouble and care —
But I hear the wind and the rain,
  And still I think of them there.

Ah, couldst thou come to me,
  Bird that I loved the best !
That I knew it was well with thee —
  Wild and weary North-West !
Wail in chimney and tree —
  Leave the dead to their rest.

OCCIDENTE.

HOW coldly sets this winter sun —
    The bitter day is wellnigh done ;
Forlorn December fares, with one
      Sad smile of last regret.
Thus from thy brief and wintry day,
O Soul ! the sunshine ebbs away :
Thus falls on thee the frozen ray,
      That lingers wanly yet :
Thus dies — how fringed with icy gold,
The clouds above yon mountain rolled !
Behind whose summit, dark and cold,
      This winter sun has set.

NOVEMBER. By L. E. B.

NOVEMBER daies are short and dour,
    And mirk, mirk fa's the night ;
Sad and alane, by the firelight dim,
   Is a dame, in weedes bedight.

For her four sons are gane frae her —
  They are gane for mony a day :
And as she listeth the wind monand,
  She grieveth, as well she may.

Twa of them were clerkly taught,
  'Mid the hills their weird they drie —
And ane is aff on the high, high land,
  And ane is farre in the South Countrie.

"O, quan sall I get letters ?" she said,
  "And quatten the newes I sall heare ?"
There came nae aunswer, nor ony sound
  But the sough o' the wind thro' the lindens dreare.

"And O, if I were sair sick !" she said,
  "And O, if I suld dee !
And my deare sons sae farre awa,
  And nane to comfort me.

"The ugsome worme wolde gnawe at my cheeke —
  Sae wolde he at my chinne :
Lang, lang or e'er my bonnie sons
  To their mither's side colde winne.

" And sairly wolde they greet to find
  Nae welcome at the hearthe —
Nae welcome but frae twa white stanes
  And a knowe o' new-turn'd earthe."

7*

MARE NON CLAUSUM.

AS one who, for a bark that nevermore
    Shall meet her gaze, still looking wearily,
Wanders, in wistful longing, on the shore
            Of the vast, desolate sea —

Thus, in vague quest of that she gathers not,
    The Soul along Life's margin lingereth —
And, musing on the inevitable lot,
            Walks by the waves of Death —

Of that drear flood, whose ne'er-surveyed extent
    This our existence ever darkens round —
Amid whose barren waste nor continent
            Nor island hath been found !

Yet Hope, Columbus-like, would fondly deem
    Far in those gloomy depths a Land may lie,
Of beauty never dreamed in human dream,
            Ne'er seen with human eye !

And when her timid feet the chill tide laves,
    Voices, nigh lost, come from that far-off Land —
Lost, in the wearying of a thousand waves
            Tumultuous on Life's strand.

How fare they — parting souls — that, ferried o'er,
See all the known receding far behind —
And catch, as yet, no glimpse of that dim shore
That waits the eternal Mind?

THE BURIAL OF THE DANE.

BLUE gulf all around us,
Blue sky overhead —
Muster all on the quarter,
We must bury the dead!

It is but a Danish sailor,
Rugged of front and form;
A common son of the forecastle,
Grizzled with sun and storm.

His name, and the strand he hailed from
We know — and there's nothing more!
But perhaps his mother is waiting
In the lonely Island of Fohr.

Still, as he lay there dying,
Reason drifting awreck,
"'Tis my watch," he would mutter,
"I must go upon deck!"

Aye, on deck — by the foremast ! —
  But watch and look-out are done ;
The Union-Jack laid o'er him,
  How quiet he lies in the sun !

Slow the ponderous engine,
  Stay the hurrying shaft !
Let the roll of the ocean
  Cradle our giant craft —
Gather around the grating,
  Carry your messmate aft !

Stand in order, and listen
  To the holiest page of prayer !
Let every foot be quiet,
  Every head be bare —
The soft trade-wind is lifting
  A hundred locks of hair.

Our captain reads the service,
  (A little spray on his cheeks,)
The grand old words of burial,
  And the trust a true heart seeks —
"We therefore commit his body
  To the deep " — and, as he speaks,

Launched from the weather railing,
  Swift as the eye can mark,
The ghastly, shotted hammock
  Plunges, away from the shark,

Down, a thousand fathoms,
  Down into the dark !

A thousand summers and winters
  The stormy Gulf shall roll
High o'er his canvas coffin, —
  But, silence to doubt and dole !
There's a quiet harbor somewhere
  For the poor a-weary soul.

Free the fettered engine,
  Speed the tireless shaft !
Loose to'gallant and topsail,
  The breeze is fair abaft !

Blue sea all around us,
  Blue sky bright o'erhead —
Every man to his duty !
  We have buried our dead.

Steamship Cahawba, at Sea, Jan. 20th, 1858.

AD NAVEM.

HOW shall we think of thee to-day —
   (For still our thoughts to thee must roam) —
Oh, ship ! that on the distant sea,
   Somewhere, art bringing Charley home ?

In airs of balm, 'mid tropic isles,
   Borne slowly on, with sleepy sail —
Or madly plunging, double-reefed,
   Against this wild northwestern gale ?

This blast that, hurrying o'er the flood,
   In turbid waves the causey whelms —
Flings white-caps o'er the shattered pier —
   And howls amid these wintry elms.

While he, this very hour perchance,
   Slow rocking in his eyrie high,
Reclined, surveys with loving glance
   The calm expanse of sea and sky.

Blow fair and strong, thou southern gale,
   The flying Gulf before thee foam !
Fill blithely every stitch of sail
   That bears the wanderer to his home.

And speed the good ship on her way —
   Ship ! that a freight dost hither bring
More welcome than the flowers of May,
   That crown this late and lingering spring.

THE RETURN OF KANE.

TOLL, tower and minster, toll
   O'er the city's ebb and flow !
Roll, muffled drum, still roll
   With solemn beat and slow ! —
A brave and a splendid soul
   Hath gone — where all shall go.

Dimmer, in gloom and dark,
   Waned the taper, day by day,
And a nation watched the spark,
   Till its fluttering died away.

Was its flame so strong and calm
   Through the dismal years of ice,
To die 'mid the orange and the palm
   And the airs of Paradise ?

Over that simple bier
   While the haughty Spaniard bows,

Grief may join in the generous tear,
  And Vengeance forget her vows.

Aye, honor the wasted form
  That a noble spirit wore —
Lightly it presses on the warm
  Spring sod of its parent shore ;
Hunger and darkness, cold and storm
  Never shall harm it more.

No more of travel and toil,
  Of Tropic or Arctic wild :
Gently, O Mother Soil,
  Take thy worn and wearied child.

Lay him — the tender and true —
  To rest with such who are gone,
Each chief of the valiant crew
  That died as our own hath done —
Let him rest with stout Sir Hugh,
  Sir Humphrey, and good Sir John.

And let grief be far remote,
  As we march from the place of death,
To the blithest note of the fife's clear throat,
  And the bugle's cheeriest breath.

Roll, stirring drum, still roll !
  Not a sign — not a sound of woe,
That a grand and a glorious soul
  Hath gone where the brave must go.

New Orleans, Feb. 24th, 1857.

AT SEA.

MIDNIGHT in drear New England,
    'Tis a driving storm of snow —
How the casement clicks and rattles,
    And the wind keeps on to blow !

For a thousand leagues of coast-line,
    In fitful flurries and starts,
The wild North-Easter is knocking
    At lonely windows and hearts.

Of a night like this, how many
    Must sit by the hearth, like me,
Hearing the stormy weather,
    And thinking of those at sea !

Of the hearts chilled through with watching,
    The eyes that wearily blink,
Through the blinding gale and snow-drift,
    For the Lights of Navesink !

How fares it, my friend, with you? —
    If I've kept your reckoning aright,
The brave old ship must be due
    On our dreary coast, to-night.

K

The fireside fades before me,
  The chamber quiet and warm —
And I see the gleam of her lanterns
  In the wild Atlantic storm.

Like a dream, 'tis all around me —
  The gale, with its steady boom,
And the crest of every roller
  Torn into mist and spume —
The sights and the sounds of Ocean
  On a night of peril and gloom.

The shroud of snow and of spoon-drift
  Driving like mad a-lee —
And the huge black hulk that wallows
  Deep in the trough of the sea.

The creak of cabin and bulkhead,
  The wail of rigging and mast —
The roar of the shrouds, as she rises
  From a deep lee-roll to the blast.

The sullen throb of the engine,
  Whose iron heart never tires —
The swarthy faces that redden
  By the glare of his caverned fires.

The binnacle slowly swaying,
  And nursing the faithful steel —
And the grizzled old quarter-master,
  His horny hands on the wheel.

I can see it — the little cabin —
  Plainly as if I were there —
The chart on the old green table,
  The book, and the empty chair.

On the deck we have trod together,
  A patient and manly form,
To and fro, by the foremast,
  Is pacing in sleet and storm.

Since her keel first struck cold water,
  By the Stormy Cape's clear Light,
'Tis little of sleep or slumber,
  Hath closed o'er that watchful sight —
And a hundred lives are hanging
  On eye and on heart to-night.

Would that to-night, beside him,
  I walked the watch on her deck,
Recalling the Legends of Ocean,
  Of ancient battle and wreck.

But the stout old craft is rolling
  A hundred leagues a-lee —
Fifty of snow-wreathed hill-side, •
  And fifty of foaming sea.

I cannot hail him, nor press him
  By the hearty and true right hand —
I can but murmur, — God bless him !
  And bring him safe to the land.

And send him the best of weather,
    That, ere many suns shall shine,
We may sit by the hearth together,
    And talk about Auld Lang Syne.

February 3d, 1859.

ALONE.

A SAD old house by the sea.
    Were we happy, I and thou,
In the days that used to be?
    There is nothing left me now

But to lie, and think of thee,
    With folded hands on my breast,
And list to the weary sea
    Sobbing itself to rest.

WAITING FOR THE SHIP.

BY C. D'W. B.

WE are ever waiting, waiting,
    Waiting for the tide to turn —
"For the train at Coventry" —
For the sluggish fire to burn —
For a far-off friend's return.

We are ever hoping, hoping,
Hoping that the wind will shift —
That success may crown our venture —
That the morning fog may lift —
That the dying may have shrift.

We are ever fearing, fearing,
Fearing lest the ship have sailed —
That the sick may ne'er recover —
That the letter was not mailed —
That the trusted firm has failed.

We are ever wishing, wishing,
Wishing we were far at sea —
That the winter were but over —
That we could but find the key —
That the prisoner were free.

Wishing, fearing, hoping, waiting,
Through life's voyage — moored at last,
Tedious doubts shall merge forever,
(Be their sources strait or vast,)
In the inevitable Past.

IN ARTICULO MORTIS.

" THE monarchy is very old," he said,
    "But it will last my time — then, after us,
The Deluge!" and meanwhile, (his thought ran
        thus,)
Our Parc au Cerfs — and Damiens to his bed
Of fire and steel.   A little, and men see
    That plague-scored lump, gasping, " *Je sens la
        Mort.*"
(Had that brief word been thine, ah, long before!
France had been happier — and 'twere well with
        thee.)
One cries, "The King is dead — long live the
        King!"
    What loyal haste in every heart prevails!
In yon deserted room a hideous thing
    Through open windows taints the soft spring gales.
Hear the Stampede of Courtiers, echoing
    Like thunder through the galleries of Versailles.

SONG OF THE ARCHANGELS.

PROLOGUE IN FAUST.

RAPHAEL.

THE sun yet sounds his ancient song,
  Exultant, 'mid the choral spheres ;
In thunder-swiftness rolled along,
  He journeys through the allotted years.
The angels strengthen in his light,
  Though none may read his mystic gaze ;
THY works, unutterably bright,
  Are fair as on the First of Days.

GABRIEL.

And swift, unutterably swift,
  Revolves the splendor of the world ;
The gleams of Aidenn glow and shift,
  The shroud of night is spread and furled.
The sea in foamy waves is hurled
  Against the rooted rocks profound ;
And rocks and seas, together whirled,
  Sweep on in their eternal round.

MICHAEL.

And storms are shouting, as in strife,
  From sea to land, from land to sea,

And weave a chain of wildest life
   Round all, in rude tempestuous glee.
There desolation flies abroad
   Before the thunder's dreaded way :
And here THY messengers, O Lord !
   Watch the sweet parting of THY day.

THE THREE.

The angels strengthen in THY sight,
   Though none may know THY wondrous ways ;
Yea, all THY works sublimely bright
   Are fair as on the First of Days.

APRÈS LA SOMMEIL.

AH, the anguish and the shame,
   And the bitter throbs of blame,
And the grief that could but weep,
All are lulled by loving sleep.
Like a summer storm it passed,
Dew and starlight followed fast —
And she lifts her lids at last,
With a tender, growing gaze,
Half of softness, half amaze —
With a rapture, low and faint,
Like some long-tormented saint
Opening recovered eyes
On a Morn of Paradise.

THE CHANGELING.

OH, mother watched my weary head,
　And father held my hand,
So I went to sleep in my little bed —
　But I woke in the Elfin-land.

How am I ever to find myself?
　When the old room shall I see?
In my cradle lieth an ugsome elf —
　And they weep, and think 'tis me.

TWILIGHT.

THE mountain wears an ominous frown,
　In the face of the troubled sky —
The woods on his crown gloom darkly down
　From their rooted hold on high —
Like the hair of a giant close shorn, I trow,
They bristle up from his shaggy brow.

8

RAPPORT.

STRANGE recognition, or of friend or foe,
  Methinks, dumb Nature hath.
This morn, as on an errand I did go,
  Pregnant of wrong and wrath —
Sliding askant, their venomous lids arow,
  Three serpents crossed my path.

May lower Malice scent out, in the vast,
  Some Sin, her foster-child?
(How the bead-eyes leered on me as they passed!)
  A shudder — then I smiled;
Ha, dost thou wink me? Sathanas, avast!
  I will be strong, but mild.

QU'IL MOURUT.

NOT a sob, not a tear be spent
  For those who fell at his side —
But a moan and a long lament
  For him — who might have died!

Who might have lain, as Harold lay,
    A King, and in state enow —
Or slept with his peers, like Roland
    In the Straits of Roncesvaux.

THE STEAM–SPIRIT.

ON SEEING A STEAM-ENGINE OF COLORED GLASSES.

WE have read, with delight and wonder,
    In the old Arabian tale,
How the Genie of smoke and vapor,
    When freed from his copper jail,

To show his cunning and mettle,
    Crept into the pot again ;
But they clapped the lid on his kettle,
    And made him a slave to men.

Still, in flue and in boiler,
    The Sprite is condemned to lurk —
To swelter, puffing and blowing —
    For still we keep him at work ;

'Mid the Armory's angry clamors,
    Forging sabre and gun —

Lifting his huge tilt-hammers
  Steadily, one by one ;

Where the mountain of cotton dwindles,
  Playing his endless parts,
'Mid the roar of reels and windles,
  And shuttles flying like darts —
Whirling a thousand spindles,
  Wasting a thousand hearts ;

Where winds and waves run frantic,
  Toiling with tireless clank,
Afar, on the wild Atlantic —
  One arm, bony and lank, .
Pumping calm and pedantic —
  T'other turning his crank.

But he is not to weld the anchor,
  Nor grind in the mill to-day —
The fettered and blinded giant
  Is shown for our sport and play.

The Steam-King's prison ? — between us,
  'Tis rather some wondrous toy,
Tinkered by Vulcan for Venus,
  When they were girl and boy ;

Or an engine built by the fairies
  For good little folks' delight —
Of amber, ruby, and crystal,
  To run of a Christmas night.

Pearl, and candy, and coral,
  Like a Baby-Inventor's dream —
Oberon trying the whistle,
  (Saucy, elfin-like scream !)
Puck, with down of the thistle,
  Busy, getting up steam.

Elves, by the dozen, clinging
  On piston and beam, pell-mell —
Tiny Titania ringing
  Hard at the ruby bell.

Some at guage and eccentric —
  Others, all in a string,
Perched upon shaft and fly-wheel,
  Whirl in a rainbow ring.

Prettiest plaything of Science !
  Fitter, methinks, to stand
(Safe from rude, mortal fingers,)
  Spinning in Fairy-Land;

'Mid the fruits of beryl and topaz,
  With emerald leaves enrolled,
That grew in Aladdin's garden,
  In the wonderful days of old —
The grapes of opal and amber,
  And the apples of garnet and gold.

LINES, KIMPOSED A BORED OF A CALIFORNY MALE–STEEMER.

BY A PARSINGER.

WAL! of all the cusséd kinveyances,
  Ef this isn't about the wust!
Nothin but rockin an rollin
  An pitchin, from the verry fust —
The ingine a groanin, and the biler
  Lyable enny minnit to bust.

Fust wun side, dum it, and then tuther!
  Till Ime dogged ef I no wot to du —
Rock away, yu darnd old kradle!
  I *wos* a baby wen I got inter *you*.

None on em seems to keer 6¼ cents
  How bad a feller may feel,
Nur to talk to him — not even the saler
  Foolin away his time on a wheel.

Thar's the capting! aint it provokin
  To see that critter, all threw the trip,
Continooally drinkin and smokin,
  Wen he orter be a mindin on his ship.

It's enuf to aggeravait a body,
   And it aint manners, I think,
To set thar takin down his toddy,
   And never askin nary parsinger to drink.

And the pusser, all he keers fur,
   Is fur to hev a time with his pals.
I say, darn sech a pusser ! jest heer him
   Flurtin and carrin on among the gals !

And wen he's tired o' that, wot follers?
   In his little cabbing thar he sets
Like a spyder, among berrils o' dollers —
   Enuf to pay a feller's dets.

That's all *they* keers for parsingers,
   Is, to git the two-hunder-
'N-fifty-dolers out of his pockit inter theirn,
   And then he may go to thunder.

Ef a feller's driv to distraxion
   In a blo, and axes wot to du,
He cant git no sort o' sattisfaxion
   Out o' none on em — capting, mait, nur crew.

Wun day I clim inter their blamed riggin,
   Jest to see wot thar wos, and in hopes
To kepe shet of em wun spell — but dog it !
   I see 2 on em comin up the ropes.

Wun on em ketcht me and hilt hold on me,
   While tother misrable cuss
Tide me up with a nasty, sticky cloze-line,
   Smellin o' tar or sumthin wuss.

Thar they kep me — darn their picturs !
   And nobody done nothin but larf,
Till I'd forkt out fur a bottle o' brandy —
   It come to $ 2½.

That's the last $ 2½
   They'll ever git out o' me,
Fur Ile travvil in a durned top-waggin,
   Afore Ile be ketcht agin to see.

EARLY POEMS.

8*

YES, all will pass away —
　　This sad and weary day,
That lingers on my path, so dull and cold,
　　Will find its home at last
　　In the returnless Past,
And join its unregretted mates of old :

　　And on some other morn
　　A brighter Babe be born —
Haply, more gentle in its task than ye,
　　Children of loveless Time,
　　All withered in your prime,
Dark Hours, that long have borne me company !

　　HATH it not erst been said,
　　(As I, methinks, have read
In some old chronicle with moral fraught,)
　　How one, in days gone by,
　　'Mid torments doomed to die —
Consoled him with the stern, yet trusty thought,

That, when of one long sun
The bitter sands had run,
Hate would have done its worst, its last on him —
Each nerve, so quick with pain,
Could never thrill again —
Nor one pang more convulse each wretched limb.

WE know not what there is,
Perchance akin to this,
Which nerves us to endure the Life we bear —
Borne, like the PILGRIM'S load,
O'er many a weary road,
Through many a path of sorrow, sin and care.

And oh ! like him could I,
These wanderings all past by,
Lay down the weight wherewith our footsteps err —
How little recked by me
Its resting-place would be,
Though 'twere, like his, a wayside sepulchre.

December, 1844.

PLACE DE LA REVOLUTION.

(10 THERMIDOR, 1794.)

" *When the wicked perish, there is shouting.*"

HERE let us stand — windows, and roofs, and
    leads,
    Alive with clinging thousands — what a scene!
And in the midst, above that sea of heads,
      Glooms the black Guillotine.

A scene like that in the Eternal City,
    When on men's hearts the Arena feasted high —
While myriads of dark faces, void of pity,
      Looked on to see them die.

How the keen Gallic eyes dilate and glare!
    The flexile brows and lips grimace and frown —
How the walls tremble to their shout, whene'er
      That heavy steel comes down!

'Tis nearly over — twenty heads have rolled,
    One after one, upon the block — while cheers,
And yells, and curses howled by hate untold,
      Rang in their dying ears.

One more is left — and now, amid a storm
  Of angry sound from that great human Hive,
They rear upright a dizened ghastly form,
      Mangled, yet still alive.

Like one emerging from a deadly swoon,
  His eyes unclose upon that living plain —
Those livid, snaky eyes ! — he shuts them soon,
      Never to ope again.

As that forlorn, last, wandering gaze they took,
  Perhaps those cruel eyes, in hopeless mood,
Sought, in their agony, one pitying look
      'Mid that vast multitude.

Sought, but in vain — inextricably mixed
  On square and street and house-top — he surveys
A hundred thousand human eyes, all fixed
      In one fierce, pitiless gaze.

Down to the plank ! the brutal headsmen tear
  Those blood-glued rags — nay, spare him need-
      less pain !
One cry ! God grant that we may never hear
      A cry like that again !

A pause — and the axe falls on Robespierre.
  That trenchant blade hath done its office well —
Hark to the mighty roar ! down, Murderer —
      Down to thy native Hell !

Again, that terrible Shout! till suburb far
   And crowded dungeon marvel what it mean —
Hurrah! and louder, louder yet, hurrah
     For the good Guillotine!

And breasts unladen heave a longer breath —
   And parting footsteps echo fast and light —
Our Foe is lodged in the strong Prison of Death!
     Paris shall sleep to-night.

THE TOMB OF COLUMBUS.[16]

AN old cathedral, with its columned roof,
    And shrines, and pictured saints.
                The sun yet lingered
On Cuzco's mountains, and the fragrant breath
Of unknown tropic flowers came o'er my path,
Wafted — how pleasantly! for I had been
Long on the seas, and their salt waveless glare
Had made green fields a longing. At the port
I left our bark, with her tired mariners;
And loitered on, amid gay-colored houses,
Through the great square, and through the narrow
    streets,
Till this old fane, inviting, stayed my steps.

While all alone, in the religious silence
And pensive spirit of the place, I stood
By the High Altar — near it, on the wall,
A tablet of plain marble met my view,
Modestly wrought — whereon an Effigy,
And a few simple words in a strange tongue,
Telling " Here lies Columbus."
                              And that niche,
That narrow space held all now left of Him
For whom the Ancient World was once too little !

Here, those illustrious Relics, doomed to wander
Like their great Tenant, — (from the holy Crypt
Of Valladolid to Moresque Seville —
Thence, voyaging West once more, to his beloved
Hispaniola — thence, for refuge, hither,) —
Had found at last their final resting-place.

But where were they — the fetters that had bound
Those patient, manly limbs ? the gift of Spain
To him who gave a world ? (in the king's name
'Twas written thus [16]) — he kept them to the last,
And charged they should lie with him in the grave.

No loftier tomb ? methought he should have lain
Enshrined in some vast pile — some gorgeous
        dome —
Reared by Castile to him who made her name
Great in the nations.   But he needs them not.
And haply, it is meeter for him thus

To rest surrounded by his own high Deeds —,
Like the great builder laid beneath the Temple
He reared.[17] " If thou wouldst view his monument,
Look round thee."
No severe majestic column,
No mountain-piled, eternal pyramid,
Such as a World might raise to its Discoverer,
Marks his repose.
But the keel-crowded port,
And the green island, and the waving palms,
And the deep murmur of a peopled city,
And the great ocean whitened with new sails,
And the wide continent stretching beyond —
All, in a voice more eloquent than words —
Inscriptions — told the story of his life.

And mine own being —
Haply, but for thee,
(If, in the tangled chain of crossed events
We shudder now to dwell upon, this soul
Had 'scaped the fatal blank of non-existence,)
Even now, I might have slaved in some old sea-port,
Bowed to the oar — or delved in Hunnish mines,
A serf — or toiled a reaper in the fields
Of " merry England " — none too merry now !

How quiet and how peaceful seemed his rest
From those long labors ? — all was calm repose.
Within, such holy stillness — but, alas !
Without, (sole stain on that great honored Name,)

A dismal sound of fetters! the chain-gang
Passing just then, with its accursèd clank.

Long by that simple tomb I lingered — long
Gazed with an awe more reverent than the pile
Heaped over King or Kaiser, could inspire.
On those calm, resolute features, ye might read,
As in a book, his strange, eventful story.
There was the Faith; the long-enduring Hope,
More than Ulyssean; the Courage high,
That fought the Infidel — and with stout heart
Clung to the shattered oar, which bore a greater
Than Cæsar and his fortunes — and when all
Cried out "we sail to death!" held firmly on
Through storm and sunshine.

                  In those furrowed lines,
As on some faithful chart, might still be traced
The weary voyaging of many years:
That restless spirit pent in narrow bounds,
Yet ever looking with unquiet eye
Beyond old land-marks — with unwearied soul
Still searching, prying into the Unknown,
And hoarding richer sea-lore — till at last
Possessed and haunted of one grand Belief —
One mighty Thought no wretchedness could lay.

The weary interval — eighteen long years,
Wandering from court to court — his Wondrous Tale
Lost in half-heeding, dull, incredulous ears;

The patient toil — the honorable want
Endured so nobly — in his threadbare coat,
Mocked by the rabble — the half-uttered jeer —
And the pert finger tapping on the head.
May Heaven accord us patience — as to him.

And now, a way-worn traveller, where, Rabida,
Thy lonely convent overlooks the sea,
(Soon to be furrowed by ten thousand keels,)
He waits, preferring no immodest suit —
A little bread and water for his boy,
O'ertasked with travel? then the welcome in,
And the good friar — saints receive his soul!

And now, (the audience gained,) at Salamanca,
Before them all, a simple mariner,
He stands, unawed by the solemnity
Of gowns and caps — with courteous, grave de-
       meanor,
And in plain words, unfolding his high purpose.

Embarked, and on the seas — at last! at last!
The toil of a long life — a Deathless Name —
The undetermined fates of all to come —
Staked on his prow — it is no little thing
Will turn aside that soul, long resolute,
(Though every heart grow faint, and every tongue
Murmur in mutiny,) to hold its course
Onward, still onward, through the pathless void,
The lone untravelled wilderness of waves —
Onward! still onward! we shall find it yet!

And next, (O sad and shameful sight!) exposed
On the high deck of a returning bark,
(Returning from that land so lately found!)
A spectacle! those aged honored limbs
Gyved like a felon's, while the hooting crowd
Sent curses in her wake.
           But when arrived,
Again exalted, favored of the crown,
And courted by the noblest — who forgets,
With his gray hairs uncovered, how he knelt
Before his royal mistress, (that great heart,
Nor insult, nor disgrace, nor chains could move,
O'ercome with kindness,) weeping like a child?

Lastly, his most resignéd Christian end ;
When, now aware of the last hour approaching,
He laid the world, so long pursued, aside ;
Forgave his foes, and setting decently
His house in order, with his latest breath
Commended that great soul to Him who gave it ;
Who rarely hath given or received a greater.

Thus loitering in the many-peopled Past,
And haunted by old thoughts, the twilight shadows
O'ertook me, still beside that resting-place
Entranced in pleasant gloom, and loth to leave.

Anon a train of dark-stoled priests swept in,
And chaunted forth old hymns.
           Was it profane
To deem their holy strain a requiem

O'er him, whose mighty ashes lay enshrined
So near his Maker? but for whom, perchance,
The sound of anthem and of chaunt sublime,
And old Te Deum's solemn majesty,
Had never echoed in the Western World.

Along each vaulted aisle the sacred tones
Floated, and swelled, and sank, and died away.
So all departed — and among the rest,
That spell upon my soul yet lingering,
I went my way — and passing to our ship,
Culled a few flowers, yet springing on the spot,
Where, wearied with long travail o'er the deep,
He landed, (so they tell,) and said the mass,
Beneath a tall and goodly Ceiba-tree,
But that is gone — and all will soon be gone.[18]

THE SPHINX.

THEY glare — those stony eyes !
    That in the fierce sun-rays
     Showered from these burning skies,
     Through untold centuries
Have kept their sleepless and unwinking gaze.

Since what unnumbered year .
     Hast thou kept watch and ward,

And o'er the buried Land of Fear
    So grimly held thy guard?
No faithless slumber snatching —
    Still couched in silence brave —
Like some fierce hound long watching
    Above her master's grave.

    No fabled Shape art thou !
    On that thought-freighted brow
And in those smooth weird lineaments we find,
    Though traced all darkly, even now,
        The relics of a Mind :
    And gather dimly thence
    A vague, half-human sense —
    The strange and sad Intelligence
        That sorrow leaves behind.

    Dost thou in anguish thus
    Still brood o'er Œdipus?
And weave enigmas to mislead anew,
    And stultify the blind
    Dull heads of human kind,
        And inly make thy moan
That, 'mid the hated crew,
    Whom thou so long couldst vex,
    Bewilder, and perplex —
Thou yet couldst find a subtler than thine own?

    Even now, methinks that those
    Dark, heavy lips, which close
    In such a stern repose,

Seem burdened with some Thought unsaid,
And hoard within their portals dread
    Some fearful Secret there —
Which to the listening earth
She may not whisper forth —
    Not even to the air !

    Of awful wonders hid
    In yon dread pyramid,
        The home of magic Fears ;
    Of chambers vast and lonely,
    Watched by the Genii only,
Who tend their Masters' long-forgotten biers ;
    And treasures that have shone
    On cavern walls alone
        For thousand, thousand years.

    Those sullen orbs wouldst thou eclipse,
    And ope those massy, tomb-like lips,
    Many a riddle thou couldst solve
    Which all blindly men revolve.

    Would She but tell ! She knows
    Of the old Pharaohs,
    Could count the Ptolemies' long line ;
Each mighty Myth's original hath seen,
Apis, Anubis — Ghosts that haunt between
    The Bestial and Divine —
(Such, He that sleeps in Philœ — He that stands
  In gloom, unworshipped, 'neath his rock-hewn
        fane —

And They who, sitting on Memnonian sands,
  Cast their long shadows o'er the desert plain :)
    Hath marked Nitocris pass,
    And Ozymandias
Deep-versed in many a dark Egyptian wile ;
    The Hebrew Boy hath eyed
    Cold to the master's bride ;
And that Medusan stare hath frozen the smile
  Of Her all love and guile,
    For whom the Cæsar sighed,
    And the World-Loser died —
  The Darling of the Nile.

THE BOOK.

A WRITTEN book before me lies.
    Therein I keep a record strange,
An ever-darkening chronicle
  Of human Fate and Change.

The list — not idly numbered o'er —
  Of those who, borne the threshold forth,
. Shall leave their footsteps never more
  Upon the sunny earth.

Strange fellowship is witnessed there,
  Strange names are mingled, side by side —

Traced coldly, or with reverent care,
  As, one by one, they died.

The gentle ones, whose angel feet
  With mine, Life's dewy pathway trod —
And they who, in the hurrying street,
  Returned a careless nod.

The friend, whose trusty heart would cling
  To mine, alike in weal or woe —
And next, the poor forgiven thing,
  That once they called my foe.

And here is one, whose sunny head
  In auburn tresses oft I curled,
And there, a Name that filled with dread
  The wonder-stricken world.

Yet lighter tharf to number all
  Whom I have marked around me fade —
To count the withered leaves that fall
  In autumn's forest shade.

Still, ever to my thoughtful eyes
Some long-forgotten form will rise.
Still I recall some buried face,
That long hath lost each human trace.

And one, who o'er each name did glance,
  (A pious, godly priest is he,)
Saith "burn thy book — full soon, perchance,
  Thine own may added be !"

9   M

And if it be, mine honest friend !
  Or now, or in life-weary age,
Think'st thou no lesson I have gained —
  No moral from its page ?

The Lovely — 'mid the haunts of mirth
  How soon their gentle reign was o'er !
The Great — how quickly from the earth
  They passed, and were no more !

And gazing here I think, since Life,
  E'en at the longest, fades so soon,
Why should we waste in care or strife
  The frail yet precious boon ?

No sermon thou didst ever preach,
  (And goodly homilies are thine !)
Hath half the power my soul to reach,
  That dwells in each poor line.

And thus, dear ghostly friend, the book,
  E'en at thy word, I will not burn —
But more thereon will rather look,
  Some gentler text to learn.

Some sad, yet far from gloomy thought —
  Some truthful lesson, pure and high —
To help us live as live we ought,
  And teach us — how to die.

PHILIP THE FREED-MAN.

I T was a barren beach on Egypt's strand,
  And near the waves, where he had breathed
    his last,
The form of one slain there by treachery
Lay stripped and mangled. On each manly limb
Somewhat of strength and beauty yet remained,
Though war, and toil, and travel, and the lapse
Of sixty years save one, had left their marks
Traced visibly.
        But the imperial head,
The close-curled locks, and grizzled beard were
    gone !
Soon to be laid before the feet of one
Who should receive with anguish, horror-struck,
Giver and gift ! — and, weeping, turn away.

The ruffian task was ended —the base crowd
Had stared its vulgar fill — and they were gone,
The murderers and the parasites — all gone.
But one yet lingered, and beside the dead,
As the last footstep died away, he knelt,
And laved its clotted wounds in the salt-sea —
Composed with care the violated frame —

Doffed his own garment, and with reverent hands
Covered the nakedness of those brave limbs.
But for a pile — a few dry boughs of wood
For him, before whose step forests had fallen,
And cities blazed ! — yet looking, sore perplexed,
He spies the wreck of an old fishing-boat,
Wasted by sun and rain — yet still enough
For a poor body, naked, unentire.

While yet he laid the ribs and pitchy planks
In such array as might be, decently,
For him, whose giant funeral pyramid
All Rome had raised — (could he have died at
       Rome) —
An old man came beside him —

                "Who art thou,
That all alone dost tend with this last service
Pompey the Great?" — He said, "I am his freed-
    man."
"Thou shalt not make this honor all thine own !
Since fate affords it, suffer me to share
Thy pious task — though I have undergone
These many years of exile and misfortune,
'Twill be one solace to have aided thee
In offering all that now remains to him,
My old commander — and the greatest, noblest,
That Rome hath ever borne !"

              They raised the body,
And tenderly, as we move one in pain,
Laid it upon the pile, in tears and silence.

And one, his friend — full soon to follow him —
(Late shipped from Cyprus with Etesian gales,)
Coasting along that desolate shore, beheld
The smoke slow rising, and the funeral pyre
Watched by a single form.

              "Who then has ended
His days, and leaves his bones upon this beach?"
He said, and added, with a sigh, "Ah, Pompey!
It may be thee!"

THE NURSE OF NERO.

WHEN he, whose name for thousand years
        hath been
But one word more for Crime and Cruelty,
Beheld his life and power, both long abused,
Draw near their end together — on each side
Armies, and provinces, and kings revolting,
A world against him — and the bitter draught,
Which he to other lips so oft had held,
Commended, with all justice, to his own —
When, through the streets of million-peopled Rome,
From door to door he went, from house to house,
And none would shelter him [19] — his aged nurse,
(For Nero's self was suckled, those fierce lips
Had drained sweet fountains — not from Agrippina,)

She, who had lulled those ominous slumbers, strove
To give him comfort — all might yet be well —
Others had been in greater straits than he.

And when at last Death clutched him — meeter prey
Those lank jaws never closed on — and dislodged
From that polluted frame the hellish sprite
That long had harbored there — when, scorpion-like,
Ringed round with foes and hate, he sought his end
With slow, unwilling hand[20] — and grieving sore —
Less for his kingdom than his fiddlestick[21] —
Expired, (two daggers planted in his throat,
And his eyes starting from his head — a terror !)
And the foul corpse was hurried under-ground —
Hers may have been the hand, the withered hand,
That all unknown "long after decked his grave
With spring and summer flowers."

THE PORTRAIT.

THOSE calm and sorrowful eyes !
        What mournful meaning lies
Within their silent depths, O broken-hearted !
        Some cold and cruel care
        Still seems to linger there —
Some trace of grief and anguish long departed.

Of tears unseen they tell,
Of trials brooked full well,
A spirit that might break, yet could not bend —
Of silent suffering borne
'Mid unrequited scorn —
And wrongs endured in patience to the end.

Oft at the silent hour,
When the Unseen hath power,
And forms of other worlds seem hovering near us —
When flickering shades that fall
Upon the darkened wall,
Advance, and then retreat as though they fear us —

When, even as now, I seem
Half in the Land of Dream,
Its mournful dwellers dimly gliding round —
Methinks I can, almost,
Discern thy hapless ghost,
And hear its timid footstep press the ground.

And thou, poor spirit, thou
Perchance art near me now,
And seekest, not in vain, some human kindness.
Oh, if thou read'st my thought,
Canst thou discover aught
Save love for thee — pity for mortal blindness?

May'st thou be far from here,
And in some happier sphere
Have long forgotten all thy gloomy part ;

The love, the gentle mirth,
Thou never knew'st on earth,
Have fallen like sunshine on that wearied heart.

Oh Love ! what lovest thou ?
The wan and careworn brow —
The faded cheek — the dark, despairing mind ?
Oh ! these are not of Thee,
Yet such would seem to be
The traces thy sweet footsteps leave behind.

DEPARTED.

A VOICE that is hushed forever —
A heart in the dull, deep clay ;
Once wildly stirred at every word
Thy cruel lips could say.

And canst thou bury the Past,
Like the dead, in its funeral pall ?
The cold, dark sneer, and the look severe —
Hast thou forgotten them all ?

All the departed one
So sadly, sweetly bore —
And how tears did rise in the gentle eyes
That now can weep no more ?

TO JOHN.

"Speak, Ancient House, oh, think'st thou yet thereon?"
GERMAN STUDENT-SONG.

ONCE more, old friend! — 'tis many a day
   Since thus beside me thou didst stand —
For I have been a weary way
   Since last I took thy hand;
And journeyed far, yet never known
A face more friendly than thine own.

By the tombstone of Memory
   We'll sit, as we were wont to do,
And trace, like Old Mortality,
   Each fading line anew.

Canst thou remember all our merry ways,
   That now are dead and gone?
Methinks it was right pleasant in those days,
   My dear old crony, John!

Once more together we will drink
   In mournful jollity,
To vanished gladness, — yet, I think,
Thy glass with mine did ever clink
   Right merrily!

9*

Aye, many a night, our vigil keeping far,
   We two did revel, answering cup for cup,
Meanwhile the Meerschaum, or mild-wreathed cigar
   Curled sweetest incense up.

Through the long night together how we read
   Old famous books — and pledged those wondrous
        men,
Whose words yet thrill, like Voices from the Dead
   Come down to earth agen.

Or pored upon the quaint and marvellous scrolls
   Of dreamy alchemist — or read the tales
Of ancient travellers, and those brave souls,
   That spread their venturous sails

For unknown lands — and sought some deep recess,
   Some old primeval forest, dark and green,
Or waved farewell across the wilderness —
   And never more were seen.

What simple fare, what modest, cheap libation
   Could then content us — Ah! what merry quips —
What genial thought — what apt, inspired quotation
   Sprang freely to our lips.

At such high tide we pondered, argued deep
   Of Life, of Destiny, of Thought profound —
Until like drowsy Wanderers, half asleep
   On the Enchanted Ground.

And when I read thee once a marvellous
  Old tale in verse, (it was thyself that bid,)
Yet somewhat of the longest — Morpheus,
  Foul fall him — closed each lid.

Thy lubbard head upon its shoulder fell —
  But I forgive thee — those were pleasant nights,
Noctes, Cœnæque ! ours, thou knowest well,
  No rude or Scythian rites.

But the wine had a perfume that is gone,
  A sparkle bright it will not have again —
Methinks thine eye was all the brighter, John,
  Yet not more friendly, then.

Still let us mingle, with a mournful pleasure,
  Hearts that not yet are touched by worldly frost,
And brood, like misers, o'er our buried treasure —
  Deep buried, yet not lost.

In cheerful sadness — yet, when we remember
  How they are gone, who sat beside each hearth,
Two ghosts, carousing in some ruined chamber,
  Could share no drearier mirth.

THE PASSING-BELL.

MARK how the bell doth toll,
          One — two — and three —
Like thee, a bodiless soul,
          Soon all shall be.

And wherefore should we mourn,
          That this dull frame
Will to the dust return,
          From whence it came?

Oft, though weary and old,
          It would not rest —
But struggles hard to hold
          The eternal guest.

It loves the pleasant earth,
          From which 'twas made ;
Still clings to care and mirth,
          Sunshine and shade.

Yet in a little while,
          (Full well I wis,)
How calmly we shall smile
          Upon all this !

And looking down, perchance,
   May, half in mirth
Yet half in pity, glance
   On this poor earth —

When Sorrows, one by one,
   Have all descended —
When the last task is done,
   The last pang ended.

And all these wondrous joys,
   These woful fears,
Shall seem like children's toys,
   Like children's tears.

OBED THE SKIPPER.

CAN ye remember, ye trusty two,
 Mates of my boyhood, so tried and true !
That sweet spring morn when we hoisted sail
To catch the breath of the southern gale —
And steered away in our slender bark,
A hundred leagues o'er the ocean dark ?

For toil or for peril what cared we ?
The flask was full, and the gale blew free.

When seas were striving hard to o'erwhelm,
Well she minded her cunning helm.
A steady eye on the flaw was cast,
A steady hand held the tiller fast.
The winds might whistle and rave their fill —
The song and the tale were never still.

The porpoise tumbled beneath our bow,
Fin and tail the shark did show,
And the gull and the petrel fluttered nigh,
Through a stormy sea and a stormy sky.
And, but for these, o'er the wide-spread sea,
No living thing save the lonely three.

And when night came down o'er the waters wide,
We were lulled to sleep by the rocking tide.
No bell we sounded — no watch we kept,
But the lantern that lazily swung while we slept.
Though the plank was hard, and the deck came nigh
As the narrow couch where we all shall lie —
Never, I ween, on a downy bed,
With curtains folded, and soft sheets spread,
Could the midnight calm on our eyelids stream
A sounder sleep or a sweeter dream.

But now, all scattered far away,
Each in a distant land, we stray.
Hardly I know if in grief or mirth
Ye are yet on the face of the sunny earth.

Many a bright spring sun hath shone,
Many a wintry blast hath blown —
But the brave old bark wherein we tost
Has left her bones on a far-off coast —
And, since that dear mad cruise, have we
Over land and over sea
Voyaged far and wearily.

Yet still, when the voice of the East is high,
And the line-storm lowers in a troubled sky,
When the forest moans, till its heavy roar
Sounds like the tide on a wild lee-shore —
My thoughts rove wandering far away
To the breaking surf and the salt sea spray —
A sail's hoarse flap in the wind I hear,
And the roar of waves is loud in mine ear.

Come around me now, companions dear,
Who love old tales by the hearth to hear —
For the night is gusty, and dark, and drear,
And the moon hath told that a storm is near.
Let the blast without raise its angriest shout,
And howl in the chimney with sullen rout —
While I tell, as fairly as tell I may,
A tale of the seas, and of times passed away.

'Twas a wild, rough day, when winds were high,
And the autumn equinox drew nigh,
Years dead and gone some thirty and three,
A gallant ship was sailing the sea.

'Tis a sight to look on, right fair and brave —
How proudly she rises from wave to wave !
With her courses furled, as she ploughs along,
And a double reef in her topsails strong.
On her hull so black a row ye might mark
Of teeth that can bite as well as bark —
Grinning full grimly on either side,
For 'twas war-time then o'er the ocean wide ;
And many a sail, both in channel and main,
Roved o'er the waters for plunder and gain.

On her privateering deck you might view
A long-sided, keen-visaged Yankee crew —
Features of marvellous shape and size,
Beet-like noses and fish-like eyes.
There was Obed the Skipper, and Peleg the mate,
And many a moe that I can't relate.
But all, as they ply the goodly trade,
Believe their eternal fortunes made.
For many a prize they have sent to shore,
And are keeping a sharp look-out for more.

But who is he, of the boyish face?
He looks like one of another race.
With his light-curled hair, and cheek so fair,
Well you had marvelled to find him there.
Yet somewhat in him but half displayed,
Showeth that of which men are made :
A firm-wreathed lip, and an eye of pride
As bright and blue as the seas they ride.

And why hath he left the pleasant shore,
For the gray salt deep, and its restless roar —
To rove with Obed on venture wild ?
That grim old man hath an only child.
To his youthful heart she has long been dear,
Long he has loved her, in hope and fear —
Yet hardly knows why he dares aspire
To win the love of her rude old sire.
Playmates from childhood, their simple flame
As yet, not even had found a name.
His voice had failed as he said " good bye,"
And a tear was trembling in Zillah's eye,
When his passionate arms were round her cast,
And he took one kiss — 'twas their first and last.
Never again shall those lips be prest,
Or that form be clasped to his loving breast.

And well and boldly full long he strove
To gain the surly old master's love.
None like William aloft could hie,
None like him could the wheel stand by.
Never a man on her deck, in sooth,
But loved the brave and the mirthful youth.

Yet howsoever he dares or tries,
Small grace hath he in the skipper's eyes.
Or if he had, on a luckless day
By an evil wind it was blown away.

A week ago, they had hailed a bark
Steering from India — the stout St. Mark.

Sooth to say, 'twas a goodly craft,
Laden full deeply fore and aft.
Already in thought the greedy crew
Are hauling her choicest stores to view —
Already are passing from hand to hand
Silks of the East and golden sand,
Teas and spices from China-land!
The boat is lowered — in the stern-sheets
His personage gruff the skipper seats.
William enters too, at his word,
And takes the helm as he steps on board.

'Twas night when they reached the stranger's side,
But the moon shone high in her autumn pride,
And her light came down so cold and keen
The Man in the Moon could be almost seen.

None with Obed mounted on deck
But the boy who followed close at his beck.
With courtesy grim the skippers meet,
Grimly smile as they bow and greet.
Long the parley, as fore and aft
They walk the deck of the captive craft.
Long in the cabin they make their stay,
And when Obed cometh at last away,
(In grave and in courteous wise they parted,)
Nor locker was oped, nor hatch was started.
Nor silk nor spice did the skipper bring,
(He hath not brought us a curséd thing!)
Save one stout chest — 'twas a grievous load —
In his private cabin right snugly stowed.

(When the cruise was o'er, and the good ship lay
Fast by the wharf in her native bay,
Cook and steward long tugged and swore
Or ever they got that chest on shore.)

But what the wonder, and rage, and grief
Of all on board, save their wily chief,
When they saw the stranger loose every sail
And glide away in the moonlight pale.
While their own swift bark, hove to at her ease,
Lay like a log on the rolling seas.

Some tale he told them — it matters not —
A letter of pass, and the Lord knows what !
But from that hour, (it was hardly strange,)
Hath fallen upon them a woful change.
The skipper weareth a threatening mien,
And a blush upon William's cheek is seen,
(For none but William had seen the gold
So slowly and grievously lugged from her hold).
He marks the boy with an evil eye
Fixed all sullenly and sly.
Seldom he cometh on deck, and then
'Tis but to growl, and to haze the men.
And on that day, with a sullen brow,
And a heart of evil, he sat below.

Full sorely he sighed, and slowly took
From his cabin locker the Holye Booke.
And now he is reading that pleasant part
Where David, (a man of the Lord's own heart,)

Bade that Uriah be left to die,
When the strife by the leaguered wall rose high.

He hath closed the Book — he hath laid it down —
And ta'en from his chest with a fretful frown
A pocket-pistol, loaded and large —
Yet it killeth not at the first discharge.

What ship is that steering up from the south ?
She carries a mighty bone in her mouth !
At her peak is a cross of glittering red —
And the pennon streams from her tall mast-head.
Mark how she rolls ! for the sea runs high,
'Tis flecked with foam like a mackerel sky.
A scud from the south comes driving fast —
And winds are raving through shroud and mast.

Obed the skipper on deck hath come,
And Ocean snuffeth the scent of rum.
Pepper-and-salt the skipper wore —
Pepper-and-salt behind and before.
Each button was big as a noddy's egg,
And the row thereof did reach to his leg.
It swelleth and tapereth o'er his thigh,
Like the shad ye catch when the stream runs high.

Seven times stalked he the length of her keel —
Seven times hath he turned on his heel.
At the stem and at the stern,
Ever the skipper taketh a turn.

A big-bellied watch in his fob doth lurk,
He pulleth it out with a vicious jerk !
Six bells are sounded — an hour hath past
Since through the glass he sighted her last.
The night is at hand — but she nears us fast !

Bitter the words he spake, and brief —
' She gains," he muttered, " shake out that reef ! "

Ear-ring and reef-point loose are cast,
And the topsail flaps on the quivering mast.
As the halliards come home, to his startled men,
" Loose the to'gallant ! " he shouts again.

'Tis done — and she flies on the snowy sail,
As a mighty bird spreads her wings to the gale.
The mast yet stands, in the tempest's roar —
But it strains as a stick never strained before !
The crew are staring in doubt and fear,
And they stare yet wider the word to hear,
Another hand must hurry aloft,
And loose yon royal, they've furled so oft.

He looked at his mates — they spoke not a word !
He looked at the crew — not a hand was stirred !
But an active step is heard at his side,
And he meets an eye of daring and pride.
And the devil within him softly said,
With a sneer, " Well, William ! are you afraid ? "

No word he uttered — or low or loud —
But sprang at once to the weather shroud.
And o'er the ratlins he climbs amain,
Through a squall that comes like a hurricane.
He has gained the cross-trees — he mounts the
   yard —
And the loosened canvas is flapping hard.
A hail is heard from his eyrie high !
A crash ! she has parted her royal-tie !
Far to leeward amid the storm
Flew the slender spar and the slender form !

Twenty feet to the boat have sprung !
Twenty hands to the braces clung !
Old Tom at the wheel lets her luff a wee,
All ready to hear them sing out " hard-a-lee ! "

But a hard rough hand, uplifted apace,
Hits old Tom in his honest face.
And a voice of anger is heard to say
" Keep fast that boat ! — keep the ship away ! "

And this was all — save a single cry,
That pierced each heart as the hull drove by,
And a fair, pale face for an instant seen,
Ere the giant billow rose high between.
But the last look on one we shall see no more,
Is stamped far deeper than all before.

In her pomp and pride the ship went by,
And left him alone on the sea — to die.

But if he sank in its soundless bed,
When the first dark surf broke o'er his head,
Or struggled long o'er his ocean-grave,
Weaker and weaker, with wave on wave —
Will ne'er be known till that Day of Dread,
The Day when the seas give up their dead!

Rough Obed follows the seas no more;
He hath built him a shingled house on the shore,
Fairly chambered, and garnished well —
Yet therein he loveth not long to dwell.

He had faced the storm, when its wildest blast
Like chaff was scattering canvas and mast.
On the deck full bold he had stood,
When the scuppers streamed, and the planks ran
      blood.

But he cannot look on that fading eye,
That is dimmer daily, he well knows why;
And the form that all slowly is wasting away,
And the cheek growing paler, day by day.

Where the sign of the Whale hangs creaking on high,
He drinks like a fish — but he's always dry!
Old Ephraim wonders what's come to pass,
And shakes his head as he fills the glass.
The by-standers whisper and stare to behold
Close Obed pay over the good red gold.
They ring it to catch the golden sound —
Heft it, and turn it, and pass it round.

Full fairly it weighs, and 'tis red to the gaze —
But it looks yet redder to him who pays !
But he eyes the change with a vacant air,
And the empty glass with an empty stare.
Nought he heeds what they look or say,
And he mutters still, as he turns away,
" They lie when they say I followed the sea —
And they lie when they say that a man follows me."

———————

.

The frost was hard in the old churchyard
As the heart that hated a famished bard.
Pickaxe and mattock, crow and spade,
A long dark trench in the earth have made —
And a narrow chest beside it is laid :
Brightly polished and quaintly built,
With its many corners, and handles gilt.
But a piteous thing lies pillowed below,
With its pale hands crossed on a breast of snow,
And its frozen tresses —— but all are hid
'Neath that never more to be opened lid.   .
'Twas a cruel dwelling for one so fair,
That cold, dark bed ! but they left her there —
Where the shades fall saddest at twilight's close,
And the long weeds wave when the night-wind
        blows —
Where the weeping willows their lean arms toss,
And the stones are gray with a century's moss.

JACK'S VISITOR.

'TIS a dull, flat common — a lonely moor,
　　Where the grass is withered and scant and
　　　poor.
In its soil so barren, swampy, and low,
The very weeds have forgotten to grow.
Poisoning the air and clouding the sky,
The monster London croucheth hard by —
(All day long from her nostrils rolled
Flames and smoke, like the giants of old) —
And the breath of her thousand fires comes forth
To taint the air, when the wind is north.

Beside it the brackish river runs,
Burdened with ships of a thousand tons.
Their black hulks float on the sluggish tide,
Or rot at anchor in reaches wide.

Robbers and murderers, half a score,
Are hung in chains on the lonely shore ;[22]
Where the sun seems only to lend his light,
To "fleer and mock" at the ghastly sight.

But the earth was hoary with frost and snow,
When here, in a house that is long laid low,

On a winter night, in the century gone,
Jack Ketch sat over his fire alone.
Weary —— for he had been hard at work —
I know not whether on Hare or Burke —
But the noose on each neck had been deftly twined,
And the bodies wavered in frost and wind.

The fire was low, the lamp burnt dim,
And the night seemed dreary, even to him.
For the storm was abroad in its wildest glee,
Rushing like mad over land and sea.
Shook each chimney and steeple high,
As the flap of its sullen wings flew by —
A sound ever followed by woe and wail,
Rending of roof and shivering of sail.

Lord ! how it blew ! — 'twas a night as wild
As that, when a mother who bore her child
Starving and shivering amid the storm,
Had stolen a blanket to keep it warm.
'Twas a thought that well might his memory greet —
He had hanged her himself in Newgate-street !

He thinks of her — and he thinks of those
He has left without to the storms and snows :
Of the chains that creak where they swing on high,
And their rags that flap as the wind sweeps by.

Was that a knock ? no, 'tis but the blast,
That shakes his door as it hurries past.

For the winds, like urchins wild in their play,
Knock naughty " doubles," and scamper away.
And the sleet and snow, and the hail and rain
Are tapping hard at his window-pane.

What ails the dog that he creeps aside
Moaning and seeking a place to hide ?
He lifts his paws as if stepping on eggs,
And his tail is hanging between his legs !

Again, a knocking ! but, as I live,
'Twas a knock that a dead-man's hand might give !

The sound was hollow, and heavy, and hard
As the oaken panel whereon it jarred.
And hark ! through the storm it cometh again,
Like the knob of some testy old gentleman's cane !

A hand without is trying the pin —
He growls in a surly tone " come in."
The door on its hinges slowly creaks
Like a wheel that hath not been oiled for weeks.
It grates half open — a man comes through,
And the wind, and the rain, and the snow come too.
But the door behind him he closeth tight,
As one who knew 'twas a bitter night.
And like one that dreadeth the dark and damp,
Draws near to the fire, and the fading lamp.

Oh Christ ! can this be a thing of earth,
That cowers and shivers upon the hearth ?

And over the wretched spark that lingers,
Spreads those frozen, skeleton fingers !

With its hollow cheek, and its glassy eye,
All ghastly and withered, shrunken and dry !
Its ribs that hardly can hide the heart,
And its blue thin lips drawn wide apart !
So shrivelled, they cannot cover the teeth,
That grin like a starving dog's beneath —
And the arms all wasted and worn to the bone —
(Might move to pity a heart of stone.)
A few bleached rags on its limbs remain,
And rusted fragments of iron chain.
Crouching low o'er the dying brands,
It rubs and stretches its bony hands !

Fain would he fly — but he sits there still —
Hand nor foot can move at his will.
Long o'er the ashes that shivering form
Strove its lean withered hands to warm —
But the air seemed death-like and icy chill,
And the storm waxed louder and colder still.

The watch-dog moans, and the lamp burns blue,
And Jack on his brow feels a deadly dew.
But his heart grew chiller than Iceland snows,
When that fearful guest from the hearth arose,
And with faltering footsteps across the room,
Hath ta'en his way through the gathering gloom,
And stayed his steps at the wainscot, where
Jack's choicest gear was arrayed with care.

On a long row of pegs, in order strung,
The trophies and perquisites neatly hung,
Picked up in his pleasant official path —
For a goodly wardrobe our hangman hath !

There was many a garment great and small,
Surtout and jacket and over-all,
Kersey and beaver and fustian stout,
Waistcoat, breeches, and roundabout.
There was many a burly and bluff top-boot,
Drawn from a highwayman's sturdy foot :
And many a pump, thin-soled and spare,
That had danced at least when it "danced i'the air."

And the shivering wretch that gropes by the wall,
Its clammy grasp hath laid on them all.
One by one, they are fingered o'er,
Till it taketh the coat that once it wore.
It hath gotten its coat, — but there it stands
Fumbling and feeling with trembling hands :
Poking before and peeping behind —
"'Tis looking for summat it cannot find !"

Why does the hangman start and stare
At the wasted knees, and the ankles bare ?
He eyes those naked limbs with a groan —
The dead-man's small-clothes are on his own !
And the dead-man, or his skeleton ghost,
Turns a stony eye on his gasping host.
A bony foot at his side doth stand —
He feels the touch of a bony hand —

Cold as an icicle — nothing more —
For he fell in a fit on the old oak floor.

The morning broke over dale and hill ;
The storm had passed, and the winds were still.
The sun was streaming the casement through,
And Jack, like a ship in a squall, "came to."
Nipping and cold was the morning air —
The garment was gone, and his legs were bare !

Next day, where togs are offered to view,
As good as new, (if you'll trust the Jew,)
At the " Grand Emporium " in Monmouth-street,
A fine display might the passenger meet !
A goodly bargain hath Israel made —
Well hath he plenished his stock in trade.

In the Times, next morn, amid lands and rents,
Moneys, mortgages, Three per Cents —
Watches stolen — purses mislaid —
Children lost, and puppy-dogs strayed —
Wedding equipments — winding sheets —
Cradles and coffins, and juggler's feats —
'Mid Patent Pills — Insurance on lives —
Wives wanting husbands, and husbands, wives —
False teeth — false eyes — false bosoms — false
       hearts —
False heads — and other yet falser parts !
With similar items, was noted down
A " nice little residence, just out of town " —
" An airy location " — " convenient for trade " —
And a " pleasant neighborhood " too, 'twas said !

Just ere the Sheriff, in solemn state,
To his dinner that evening sate —
" Mr. Ketch," said the footman tall,
" Vaits his vorship vithin the hall."
A shocking bad hat is doffed to the ground,
And Jack bows low, as in duty bound ;
And tenders in form a resignation
Of his useful, exalted — exalting station.

The Sheriff hears with a heavy heart,
Loth from his trusty friend to part,
Who had served him long, and with right good-will—
'Twas not that the office was hard to fill !
He yields the point, though with evil grace —
" There were gemmen enough who would like the
          place."
And from that hour, on the Thames' foul shore,
Jack Ketch in his haunts was seen no more.

And oh, if the wisdom so dearly bought
In the dark, dark lesson the past hath taught —
If the slighted counsels of Love and Worth,
And the tears of angels weeping for earth,
And the prayers of the just were not all in vain —
We ne'er should look on his like again !

DIES IRÆ.

DAY of wrath! that awful day,
Earth in ashes sinks away!
David and the Sibyl say.

Oh! what terror will arise,
When the Judge shall leave the skies,
All to mark with searching eyes!

And the trumpet's wondrous sound
Through the nations under-ground
Gathers all the throne around.

Death shall shudder — Nature then
Tremble, as she wakes agen,
Answering to the Judge of men.

Forth is brought the volume penned,
Wherein all things are contained,
Whence the world shall be arraigned.

Therefore, when the Judge shall reign,
All that's hidden shall be plain,
Nought shall unavengéd remain.

What then, wretched, shall I say,
Or what intercessor pray,
When the just may scarce find stay.

King of awful majesty!
Who thy chosen savest free,
Save me, Fount of Piety!

Jesus, thou hast not forgot
Me, the cause of thy sad lot;
In that day, oh, lose me not!

Seeking me, thou satst in pain,
On the cross for me hast lain:
May such anguish not be vain!

Judge of vengeance! righteous King!
Gift of thy remission bring,
Ere the day of reckoning.

Like a wretch condemned I groan,
Red with guilt my face is shown;
Spare me kneeling at thy throne!

Thou, who pitiedst Mary's grief,
And didst hear the dying thief,
Me hast also given relief.

All unworthy is my prayer,
But thou, good, in mercy spare
Flames eternal from my share.

10*   o

'Mid thy flock then let me stand,
Parted from the goats' foul band,
Placing me on thy right hand.

When th' accursed, put to shame,
Are consigned to fiercest flame,
With thy Blessed call my name.

Bowed and suppliant I bend,
Crushed like dust my heart I rend;
Take thou care, Lord! of mine end.

TO ———

THOU gavest me a fair red rose,
  Thou gavest me a violet —
I thought them poor and pale to those
  In thy beloved features met.

No rose of June could e'er eclipse
The glory of those budding lips —

And the flower that gathers its virgin hue
  From the gleam of the summer skies,
Hath ne'er so lovely and tender a blue
  As beams from thine own sweet eyes.

ÆGRI SOMNIA.

LAST night, in sad and troubled dreams,
　　Again thy spirit crossed my sleep —
That strange, unquiet slumber seems
　　No other form to keep.

Methought I wandered forth once more,
　　Beneath the dying moon's pale face,
And stood, as I have stood before,
　　At the old trysting-place.

Long watching — but thou cam'st at last,
　　No longer proud — no longer cold —
And those dear arms were round me cast,
　　As kindly as of old.

And that dear lip sought gently mine,
　　In mild and tender accents breaking —
Ah, * * * * * ! if that dream divine
　　Had never known a waking !

ANACREONTIC.

"It is worth the labor, saith Plotinus, to consider well of Love, whether it be a god or a divell, or passion of the minde, or partly god, partly divell, partly passion. * * * * * Give me leave then (to refresh my muse a little and my weary readers) to expatiate in this delightsome field, ' hoc delicia-rum campo,' as Fonseca terms it, to season a surly discourse with a more pleasing aspersion of love-matters. * * * * * And there be those, without question, that are more willing to reade such toyes, then I am to write."
— BURTON'S ANATOMY OF MELANCHOLY.

EROS, graceless Wanton ! thou
Wast mine earliest playfellow.
Well I knew thee, roguish Elf !
When an infant like thyself.
And thou still must needs abide
Clinging wilful to my side.

Every other frolic mate
Long has grown to man's estate —
Other childish sports have past,
Other toys aside are cast —
One alone could yet remain ;
'Tis the vainest of the vain !

Still this fond and foolish heart
Must enact a childish part,

And in Beauty's Presence still
Feel its wonted boyish thrill.
Chide thee — shun thee as I may,
Thou hast ever had thy way ;
Many a subtle snare hast laid —
Many a wanton trick hast played.
E'en at Learning's council sage,
Thou hast perched upon the page,
(Latin could not mar thy glee,
Greek was never Greek to thee,)
And when Wisdom should prevail,
Told me many a roguish tale,
Many a scene of vanished Love —
Dicte's cave and Ida's grove,
And the mountain fringed with fir,
And the paths beloved of Her,
Who the sleeping hunter eyed
Couched on Latmos' shaggy side.
Of each old enchanted spot —
Tyrian mead — Egerian grot —
Each dim haunt, remembered yet,
Where mortal with Immortal met —
Darksome glen and sunny glade —
And all the pranks that Sylvan played.

One kind turn I owe thee — one
Kindly office thou hast done.
Ne'er shall I forget the hour,
When thy soft-persuading power
Led my footsteps, roving wide,
To the Sleeping Beauty's side.

Wearied, like a child from play,
Lightly slumbering, there she lay.
Half a crime though it might seem
To disturb so sweet a dream —
Yet, with tender, reverent soul,
Softly to her side I stole,
And the only means did take
Such a slumber e'er should wake.

Like a half-awakened child,
Gently then she moved and smiled ;
With a soft and wondering glance —
Such as Gyneth wore, perchance,
When she oped her lovely eyes
From the sleep of centuries.

THE ADIEU.

SWEET Falsehoods, fare ye well !
   That may not longer dwell
In this fond heart, dear paramours of Youth !
   A cold, unloving bride
   Is ever at my side —
Yet who so pure, so beautiful as Truth ?

   Long hath she sought my side,
   And would not be denied,

Till, all perforce, she won my spirit o'er —
 And though her glances be
 But hard and stern to me,
At every step I love her more and more.

LONG AGO.

WHEN at eve I sit alone,
 Thinking on the Past and Gone —
While the clock, with drowsy finger,
Marks how long the minutes linger —
And the embers, dimly burning,
Tell of Life to Dust returning —
Then my lonely chair around,
With a quiet, mournful sound,
With a murmur soft and low,
Come the Ghosts of Long Ago.

One by one, I count them o'er,
Voices, that are heard no more,
Tears, that loving cheeks have wet,
Words, whose music lingers yet —
Holy faces, pale and fair,
Shadowy locks of waving hair —
Happy sighs and whispers dear,
Songs forgotten many a year, —

Lips of dewy fragrance — eyes
Brighter, bluer than the skies —
Odors breathed from Paradise.

And the gentle shadows glide
Softly murmuring at my side,
Till the long unfriended day,
All forgotten, fades away.

Thus, when I am all alone,
Dreaming o'er the Past and Gone,
All around me, sad and slow,
Come the Ghosts of Long Ago.

NOTES.

NOTES.

A PORTION of this book was issued, in the third year of the war, under the title of "Lyrics of a Day, or Newspaper Poetry, by a Volunteer in the U. S. Service," with the following Preface,

NOTE TO THE ORIGINAL EDITION.

" All the pieces in this volume have been printed heretofore — mostly in the daily papers. Some of them, rather trivial, are included because of their popularity. Indeed all those on war and polity seem to me but ephemeral expressions — *suspiria, risus, elatio* — of the great national Passion, in its several phases. They are spray, as it were, flung up by the strong Tide-Rip of Public Trouble, and present the Time more nearly, perhaps, than they do the writer. Penned, for the most part, on occasion, from day to day, (and often literally *currente calamo*,) they may well have admitted instances of diffuseness, contradiction, or repetition.

On overlooking them, I find almost nothing, in substance, to omit or qualify. I have chanted of Treason and Slavery, sometimes fancifully or passionately, perhaps — always fairly, in effect, I hope. Let us give the latter of these Twin Gentlemen his due, whatever that may be.

Can a slave-holder be a good man? Assuredly, to my thinking — especially where manumission is impracticable, by reason of law or popular violence. But, so far as I have seen, he is good in spite of his slave-holding, not because of it. Justice, humanity, regard to natural right — these can hardly be credited to a *status*, the single condition of which is the allowed infraction of them. They belong to the man, not to the business. Thus much for those friends of mine who are, or have been slave-holders, and whose natural goodness could convert a relation so injurious in its essence, and often so horrible in its concomitants, into something at least not absolutely shocking the senses, nor quite precluding the interchange of kindly feeling. Thus much, too, for those of us, who, travelling or residing in slave-regions, have also certainly been amenable to whatever blame may attach to the naked fact of using slave-services.

But how suddenly and thoroughly an ill usage may pervert the best feelings, is patent enough. What travellers were those, in Java, who, in their first morning's ride, had such a shock on seeing the abject prostration of all the natives they encountered? They soon got bravely over it, however — for, on their way home, meeting a couple of Chineses, who did *not* fling themselves on their faces, they were vastly scandalized at the omission, and, as they tell us, exclaimed with one voice, "Confound the impudence of those fellows!" So easy is it to reconcile one's self to whatever may be held as "the thing," and so natural to think empirically. It is a system, and its results, average or extreme, not individuals, that I have dealt with.

True, it is only of late that any American (or, for the matter of that, any European) could, with the least personal consistency, assail the system — always excepting a very few of the original emancipationists, who, from the first, grimly and grandly pretermitted all use of the *products of slave-labor*. For the rest of us, we have been art and part — accessaries before and after the fact. It is now these many years that we have held an uncommonly large Candle (saving your presence) to the Devil. It is going out, and the snuff and smoke come under our noses pretty strongly — but he won't let us drop it, as long as a spark remains to light his work withal. Let us bear it as we may, and not make matters worse by trying to puff it alight again.

'Tis certain, we can hardly lay claim to the initiation of what has turned out such a sturdy contest of right against wrong. I dare say we should have gone on, *in sæcula*, in the old way, had not Aphrosyné, that wild-eyed angel, (who, at the worst pinch, always does the will of the Gods,) descended to fire the Southern Heart. A sublime *vis inertiæ*, three years ago, on a point of abstract right, was our earliest political merit. Since then, by sacrifices without precedent, in defence of the same, and by a readiness to share the burden of expiation and reform, the Nation, at last, has fairly earned the right to speak. Here is one of its voices — would it were nearer to

> ' The height of this great argument.' "

Note 1. Page 2.

The Flag-ship of Richard I.

Note 4. Page 42.

Chicama-uga.

Note 5. Page 46.

" *Des habits bleus par la victoire usés.*"

Note 6. Page 51.

" The finest thing I ever saw was a live American eagle, carried by the 8th Wisconsin, in the place of a flag. It would fly off over the enemy during the hottest of the fight, then would return and seat himself upon his pole, clap his pinions, shake his head and start again. Many and hearty were the cheers that arose from our lines as the old fellow would sail around, first to the right, then to the left, and always return to his post, regardless of the storm of leaden hail that was around him. Something seemed to tell us that that battle was to result in our favor, and when the order was given to charge, every man went at them with fixed bayonets, and the enemy scattered in all directions, leaving us in possession of the battle-field." — *Letter from an Illinois Volunteer.*

"We give below a short account of this noble bird, written by a staff officer of that regiment : —

'Allow me to introduce to you an object of interest, the "Old Eagle." He may be seen a little above the heads of the soldiers, close by the flag. This position of honor is never disallowed him. The perch upon which he sits is borne by a young man in Company C, to whom his safe keeping is exclusively intrusted. . . . . He was taken from the nest, in Chippeway county, Wisconsin, July, 1861, by a Chippeway Indian, and by him presented to a farmer near by. He was subsequently bought by a citizen of Eau Claire, who presented him to Company C, 8th Regiment. The present excellent commander of that company, Capt. Wolf, gave him the name of "Abe," the name by which he is uniformly known among us, and to which only he deigns to answer. When the regiment marched into Camp Randall, the instant the men began to cheer, he spread his wings, and taking one of the small flags attached to his perch in his beak, he remained in that position until borne to the quarters of the late Col. Murphy. Ever since he was mustered into the service, his wings have been instantly outstretched on the occasion of any cheering by the regiment. To similar demonstrations in adjacent regiments he pays no regard. . . . . . He has been in all the battles of the regiment, equally exposed with the troops. At the battle of Farmington, May 9th, 1862, the men were ordered to lay down. The instant they did so, it was impossible to keep him on his perch. He insisted on being protected as well as they, and when liberated, flattened himself on the ground, and there remained till the men arose, when with outspread wings he resumed his place of peril and held it to the close of the contest.

'At the battle of Corinth, the Rebel Gen. Price having discovered him, ordered his men to be sure and take him if they could not kill him, adding that he had rather get that bird than the whole brigade. Upon the whole he is a magnificent bird, and, I opine, will erelong spread his wings in triumph over other sections of now disloyal territory.'

"Since this paragraph was written, our Eagle has, with his regiment, served out his term of enlistment, and at its close was presented to Governor Lewis of Wisconsin. He now rests on his laurels, living in apartments fitted up expressly for him in the State House Park at Madison.

"Governor Lewis has consented to his coming to our Great Northwestern Sanitary Fair in May, to exhibit himself for the benefit of the sick and wounded soldiers, — his companions in arms."— *History of the Eagle of the 8th Wisconsin.*

NOTE 7. Page 56.

"The storming party looked in vain for the support which had been promised it. The brigade which had been ordered to follow it hesitated. Finally, all but one of the 150 got discouraged, and sought the shelter of a deep ravine. William Trogden, a private of Company B, 8th Missouri, refused to retrace a single step. He was color-bearer of the storming party. When his comrades left him, he dug a hole in the ground with his bayonet, planted his flag-staff in it, within twenty yards of the enemy's rifle-pits, and sat down by the side of his banner, where he remained all day."— *Report of the Assault on Vicksburg.*

NOTE 8. Page 80.

In Zollicoffer's camp, it seems, were found quantities of children's clothes, plundered from loyal houses by the Rebels, and carefully preserved for the use of their own offspring.

NOTE 9. Page 84.

Somewhere in Tennessee, it appears, the bloodhounds trained to hunt slaves, by a very natural and easy conversion, came to be used for the business of catching fugitive Unionists; whereupon, our Western soldiers, (who are hard to please,) on occupying that neighborhood, took to killing them off — to the great disgust of all chivalrous and conservative hearts, and to the manifest damage and infraction of the Constitution.

NOTE 10. Page 86.

"It is the dirtiest chimney that has been on fire this century — the only way is to let it burn itself out."

NOTE 11. Page 88.

"How different," exclaims Mohammed, "is the Tree Al-Accoub from the Abodes of Paradise! We have planted it for the torment of the wicked."

This Tree, say the Islamite Doctors, had its root in hell, and bore for fruit devils' heads, filled with ashes.

NOTE 12. Page 89.

The Ceiba of San Antonio. There are others even more striking.

NOTE 13. Page 122.

"His temperament was cheerful. At table, the pleasures of which in moderation were his only relaxation, he was always animated and merry; and this jocoseness was partly natural, partly intentional. In the darkest hours of his country's trial, he affected a serenity he was far from feeling; so that his apparent gayety at momentous epochs was even censured by dullards, who could not comprehend its philosophy, nor applaud the flippancy of William the Silent. He went through life bearing the load of a people's sorrows with a smiling face." —*Motley's Rise of the Dutch Republic.*

Perhaps a lively national sense of humor is one of the surest exponents of advanced civilization. Certainly a grim sullenness and fierceness have been the leading traits of the Rebellion for Slavery; while Freedom, like a Brave at the stake, has gone through her long agony with a smile and a jest ever on her lips.

Note 14. Page 179.

The charm of Solomon against elation in prosperity and dejection in adversity.

Note 15. Page 183.

" But thee, *Columbus,* how can I but remember? but loue? but admire? Sweetly may those bones rest, sometimes the Pillars of that Temple where so diuine a spirit resided ; which neyther want of former example, nor publike discouragements of domesticall or forren states, nor priuate insultations of prowd Spaniards, nor length of time (which usually deuoureth the best resolutions) nor the vnequal Plaines of huge vnknowne Seas, nor grassie fields in Neptune's lap, nor importunate whisperings, murmurings, threatenings of enraged companions, could daunt : O name *Colon,* worthy to be named vnto the world's end, which to the world's end hast conducted *Colonies:* or may I call thee *Colombo* for thy *Doue-like simplicitie* and patience? the true *Colonna* or Pillar, whereon our knowledge of this new world is founded, the true *Christopher* which, with more than Giant-like force and fortitude hast carried Christ his name and religion, through vnknowne Seas, to vnknowne Lands." — *Purchas his Pilgrimage.*

Note 16. Page 184.

"Por Castilla y por Leon
Nuevo mundo hallo Colon."

NOTE 17. Page 185.

Wren in St. Paul's.

> ".... si monumentum queris,
> Circumspice."

NOTE 18. Page 189.

I believe there is no evidence that Columbus ever landed at the harbor of Havana — but the people of that city cling to the idea with a creditable pertinacity.

NOTE 19. Page 197.

Lives of the XII Cæsars.

NOTE 20. Page 198.

Comparisons are proverbially odious ! (would that Plutarch had thought so !) but we cannot refrain from remarking some singular coincidences in the lives of two of the worst of men. "Quam vellem nescire literas !" — said the grandson of the high-souled Germanicus, when the first death-warrant was presented to him. (Cortés said the same.) Robespierre, the virtuous, the incorruptible, forsakes the chair of office rather than be accessary to the shedding of blood. In their last hours the resemblance becomes yet closer. Each, when all was over, attempted suicide, but so clumsily and unskilfully, that others were compelled to finish what their trembling hands had failed to accomplish.

NOTE 21. Page 198.

"He continually exclaimed, 'Alas ! what a musician is about to perish !'" — TACITUS.

NOTE 22. Page 217.

This tasteful and salutary practice is of ancient date, and would seem to have been originally founded on the idea that

—(to use the quaint words of Mr. Justice Blackstone) — "it is a comfortable sight to the relations and friends of the deceased."

Further to promote this "comfortable" frame of mind, it was also customary for the relations and friends aforesaid to drag the criminal by a long rope to the place of execution, — a process ingeniously and kindly devised to soothe their bereaved and excited feelings.

The description which old Plowden (in his barbarous law-French) cites from Bromely, is too curious to be omitted.

". . . . quaunt le felon fuit troue culpable en appel de murder, que le auncyant usage fuyt, que touts ceux del sanke (sang) cesty que fuyt murder traheront le felon per longe corde al execution, quel use fuit foundue sur le perd q tout le sank auoit pur le murder del un de eux, et pur lour reuengement, et le amour que ils auoyent a luy tue, ceo fuit use." — II HENRY 4, 12.

THE END.

Cambridge : Stereotyped and Printed by Welch, Bigelow, & Co.

www.ingramcontent.com/pod-product-compliance
Lightning Source LLC
Chambersburg PA
CBHW030806020726
47499CB00006B/1781